For My Family

For My Family

Mickey Bahr

2008

Tiger Publishers

Published in the United States of America by
Tiger Publishers
6632 Landover Circle
Tallahassee, FL 32317
E-mail: tigerpublishers@gmail.com.

FIRST EDITION

ISBN 978-0-6152-4336-8
EAN 53495

The text of this book is set in 12-point Book Antiqua.
Manufactured in the United States of America

From the journals of Mickey J. Bahr

PART I

I have found my beast.

Most would consider it an accomplishment to tame a beast. Whatever its size, whether it's a snake or a dragon, beasts are wild creatures. They roam in the depths of darkness, lurching around for anything to harm. In a bottle of purified water, even today there are bacteria destined to make you sick. In the streets and down the alleys rapists and murderers sit, waiting for anyone to step in. Hurricanes flood cities, starting fires that burn the flesh of bodies later to just float around aimlessly.

Every building has its breaking point. Every rapist and murderer must evade the police. No matter how much you boil water, some disease always remains.

These are beasts, impossible to tame and altogether inconceivable to hinder growth. The beasts that roam in the depths of darkness are what cause fear and hysteria among many. They can try to stop a beast, but it only consumes their soul. It is a wasted effort.

These are the fools: they have not learned from the past; they repeat the mistakes of the past; they make themselves an item of the past. All the while, their beast lives on.

I have found my beast.

In one night of heavy rain, the stream behind my house has finally filled. For the first time to my eyes, water flows around the small bend, over the tree root, gets skinny, then wide, and then opens to a little dip in which the water trickles with a soothing splash. The splashes enter a small widening of the stream with just enough depth to wade (but I wouldn't dream of stepping in this water; no doubt it is straight from the heavens themselves, but all that water started on the ground somewhere).

Within the confines of this small pond, fish swim. Where they come from I know not, but I do know the stream ends up in some drain somewhere. Perhaps someday I will follow it, but I will not today. Today there are fish, different kinds too. There are the typical pond guppies, a thousand of them. There are a couple strange white fish I've never seen before.

I have two fish aquariums. One is a twenty-gallon; it sits on top of a ten-gallon tank in this iron framing made for serving dinner.

The bottom tank has three albino catfish (bottom-feeders), some black mollies, and then two other strange fish my brother left in the tank.

I don't know if I really like fish, but I promised to take care of them for my brother. So each day I get up and feed the fish, and then in the evening I feed them again.

"Twice a day for food, and clean the tanks at least six times a year."

This is the advice I was left with from my brother.

I truly am excited when my stream has fish in it. Unfortunately, I know their fate. As the summer changes to fall, as it does each year, the water will dry up, sealing the death of a thousand flapping minnows.

One thing I have learned is to forget the minnows. They are not important. They're just small boring fish that all look alike and swim together. It is disgusting.

The other fish are the ones to worry about; those strange white fish, and today there are some black fish with whiskers. Catfish! But they're so small.

These are my beasts.

They all come over pretty easily. One even swims right into my net when I stick it into the water. They want to come with me.

I have a bucket filled with the stream water. As each one comes to me, I quickly plop it right into the bucket, where it retreats to the bottom out of instinct.

One, two, three, four, five.

One more to go for six. Six is a good number, a perfect number.

This one seems a little more difficult. As it hides under a leaf, I question my usual approach of sticking the net in the water and having the fish come to me. It looks like this is one fish I will have to get myself.

In the middle of the pond there's a rock sticking just out of the water. It's small at the top, but as it goes down it gets larger. It seems stable enough.

I tap my left foot on it to be sure, slowly putting more and more pressure. It sticks.

I take my net and stick it just on the surface of the water. The black catfish moves from the shadows.

I see its eyes for the first time. They are truly stunning. Who could have ever guessed in a body as small and dark as its body, there would be two blue diamonds sticking for everyone to see? It's the strangest color I've ever seen; a glossy blue covered by this murky grey cloud. I'm trapped in a gaze.

Slowly I move to touch it with my hand. My foot slips.

SPLASH!

I struggle to escape the dark water but I can't seem to stand up. I take in a deep breath, and water fills my lungs. I scramble to the side and cough out the poison. Finally I am able to breathe without a rasp.

I stand up and shake off the mud. A piece plops into the water; there's the fish. Those eyes looking at me, through my net. I take the net. The fish is still. I slide it into the bucket where one of the catfish has already floated to the top.

Five is a good number.

I have now acquired a beast to tame -- five of them it would seem. I bring the bucket inside the house and set it aside. The fish need time to adjust to the new temperature of a modern air-conditioned society.

I walk out to the shed. It's a nice shed -- very useful for tasks. Today I've decided to make a wooden boat to float down the stream. I gather various scrap pieces of wood and in thirty minutes make what looks to be more like a log that has been struck by lightning; the bark charred away leaving only a malformed structure of some sort.

I jog to the bend in the stream and drop my boat in the water. Within seconds it flips upside down and tumbles, banging off the side bank every once in a while. Well, at least it floated. I grab it out of the water, shake it off, and toss it into the forest beyond.

I jog back into my house. Back inside I glance at the clock and then at the bucket.

I always did think four was a better number anyway.

I decide to be a little more aggressive this time. I lurch over the bucket and then snatch my hand into the water. I squeeze and move what I've grabbed to the bottom fish tank. I guess I squeezed too hard.

Three is a better number anyway.

Was it even worth trying to save them? I suppose three living fish are better than six dead ones. I decide to just pour the bucket into the tank. The water level was low anyway. As a cloud of dust stirs underneath, my three beasts swim to prowl in the bottom. I watch for five minutes. They don't move; task accomplished!

I might have been but five years of age when my father and brother brought home the first fish aquarium. It was a hexagonal-shaped three-gallon tank. The rocks were green, and it had one giant orange stone and an orange plant that "grew" to the top. At five years of age, I believed anything was alive. But of course, being of this young age, I questioned their intentions.

"What's that for?" and "Can the fish get out?" I asked through the steps of their initial setup.

After answering each of my questions, all two hundred and thirty six of them, my brother plopped the two bright orange goldfish into the tank. They blended nicely with the plant. And after about five minutes, we all got bored with it and walked away. The tank sat alone on the kitchen counter.

It was a moving gift our parents had bought my brother and I. They had promised us that if neither of us complained during the move, they would reward us with fish. Since we were only moving about fifteen miles in town, I only cried six times and my brother broke down about three. It wasn't that much of a burden for our parents, so they decided they could settle for fish. I mean, it's not like we were asking for a dog.

Fish were easy. All you had to do was feed them once in the morning and then once at night, and then of course you had to clean the tanks, which may take up a Saturday morning here or there, but it's better when compared with walking a dog. Fish don't walk, they don't bite (unless you brush your finger across the top of the water like it's food), and they don't urinate on the sofa. Like I said, fish were an easy choice for my parents.

Later that day I decided the fish looked a little hungry, so I dropped some food in. Opening the container and then flipping it upside down doesn't work that well I guess. The two fish were dead within the hour. Too bad, so sad. My dad waited a while to make a trip to the pet store. He thought it would be a good learning tool for us, one of those life lessons.

The funny thing is, my brother didn't care that much. I mean, sure he was disappointed, but he didn't take it out on me. He saw it as a failure on his part. So from that moment on he made it his goal to train me in the basics of fish care. That's what older brothers are for.

My dad told him to make sure the tanks stay clean for guests. So in light of this newly given responsibility, my brother pondered his options. Clean the tanks yourself, or give it to someone else? Hmm...I wonder. That's what younger brothers are for.

Settling into a new house was quite an impressive experience at such a young age. While I had yet to establish myself in the world, nor had I the ability to retain much of a long-term memory, I was young. Everything is much bigger when you're tiny. But I wasn't too worried about it. Mom and Dad were always there.

This house would be the place I made all of my greatest memories. Family gatherings, breakfasts before school starts, watching those great cartoon TV shows on the weekends, and starting to shave; these were all the things I would get to have memories of in this house. I was in a house, why complain? No, it wasn't just a house; it was a home, a place of love, a place of my future. It was an exciting thought. Of course I didn't realize any of this besides the obvious wonder at the time.

A young family settling in the newly developed neighborhood, we were most excited about the land. My parents each wanted certain qualities in the house. Of course they thought it wouldn't be their last home, so they had to settle with some things. They got the front porch...sort of. They got the paved driveway...sort of. They got the brick home...sort of. They sort of got some of their sorted hopes. To be honest, it didn't matter much to me. All I cared about was one thing: I would finally have my own room.

I like my room. It's just right for me. Four sides, one ceiling (with a five-bladed, white fan), and one floor carpeted with a plush golden forest. I fell off my bed once to find my face flat against the floor. What a great night of sleep.

It's amazing how something composed of so many little fibers can feel only like a flat piece of fabric on your feet.

Back on my bed now, I decide to read a book. I reach to the floor beneath my bed and feel for a book. There are four. I swipe my hand around until I feel a good sized one. I find one book that's not too thick or too large; it's perfect. What do we have here?

Hamlet.

Well then *Hamlet* it will be. What a classic play. Well, I've been told it's a classic, so I go along with it. And now I am here reading, in my bed, in the room that I like.

Slowly, as my eyes drift over the words, I begin to nod off. It's a pity. I like Shakespeare.

I made a sword once from a pocketknife and a large branch. Well, it wasn't that large of a branch, only about two feet long and an inch thick, but it's served its purpose well.

I was a child with an imagination waiting to be filled. My pen was yet to be lifted, so I decided to lift it myself.

I took my knife and scraped against the wood. It cut without resistance. Slowly moving my knife from one end to the other, I sharpened the stick to a point. It's still sharp today.

As I played throughout that day, it pierced into my head, filling my memories with violence. I have never opposed violence. In fact many times I find it to be quite interesting, but it still disturbs me late at night.

I'll toss and I'll turn, just as I am now. I awaken with sweat dripping off my face. There's nothing I can do about it. I'll have to take a shower before I do anything important, not that my calendar is packed 8 to 8.

A flash of memory runs through my head. The stick. I was killed.

I dreamed of a man, a very evil man. He's eyes were heavy set, deep into his face, much like my own. His brooded with a dark brown fury.

He had something. A girl. A little girl no more than eight years old. He held her with the stick to her neck, my stick.

I was in a chair. Was I tied down? I was, but somehow I got free.

I charged at the man with all my might, raising my hand to stop him. When my body was touching his, I looked down to see the dagger pierced in my heart.

As I staggered away, the stick slowly pulled from my chest. I stumbled back to the chair.

He grabbed the girl. There was nothing I could do, but I still needed to make an attempt.

I pushed one foot into the floor, but then the man was right in front of me. He gripped the dagger in his left hand and reared it bending his arm back. In one jerk the stick broke through my jaw and jammed up into my brain. I felt the pressure, but I felt no pain. It was kind of like getting a tooth pulled.

As I lay with my head slouched, the man with the deep-set, brown eyes walked slowly into the coming darkness, dragging the girl all the way.

This is how I dream. Normally I might question why I have a dream like this, but ever since the night of heavy rain, these violent dreams have been occurring more and more frequently. I suppose it is only a phase my mind is going though, and I'll hopefully get over it in time.

But still, when I awake to see the ridged dagger sitting on my dresser, I question my sanity. It's comical, but it appears to have blood on its sharpened point.

I rub my eyes and the hallucination disappears. I really should try to get more sleep at night. It is just, I can't control my mind. My body can be dead and heavy as a boulder, but my mind still tempts me to run around my house. There's nothing I can do about it.

I've tried everything this one pamphlet suggested. One of the ideas was comical. It advised to do something "soothing" before lying down to sleep. I suppose it's not that funny, but I've never really done anything relaxing before bed. It's my own fault.

Each night I sit awake and ponder the day's occurrences. Freud thinks this is supposed to occur during sleep. I can't sleep, so I disagree.

There's no point in continuing to lie on my bed, so I walk back to the fish aquariums. Out of my room, down the hallway, and straight through the living room I walk.

The lights still linger on in the tanks, as it is turning to night outside.

I grab the multicolored food-flakes the fish supposedly love to eat (personally they're kind of stale and dry). I take a pinch for the top tank and drop it in. It spreads out across the top and begins to sink to the bottom. I crouch down to drop some in the bottom.

My black mollies aren't anywhere to be found in the tank. I guess that's what I get for dropping in the beasts.

I take a pinch more of food and drop it to the water. It sits on the top and doesn't spread at all. I need to clean the tank; the filter has stopped pumping water. The food sinks to one side of the tank, but none of the catfish move.

I flip on the television, but nothing catches my eye. After five minutes of Spanish soap operas, I decide to call a friend.

I walk to my room and search around until I find my phone. I flip it open and press and hold the seven button. Kaitlyn's name pops up and a dial tone soon kicks in.

"Hello?" she says.

"Hey, it's me," I reply.

After thirty minutes of darting conversation, I invite her over to hang for a little while.

"Sounds wonderful!" she concludes after weighing her options over the phone.

"I can sit at home and do nothing, or I can just be bored with you."

Sarcasm is a wonderful thing. It's obvious we're exciting people. Instead, we just laugh off the lack of events in our lives.

"I'll be over in fifteen!" Kaitlyn says right before hanging up.

"Good-bye?"

Dial tone.

I flip the television back on and drift to sleep on the couch. Just as a thought forms in my mind, I'm shot awake by the ring of my phone. I pick up. She's outside. I go to the door and let her in.

"Hello there," she says as she steps inside.

"Hey," I reply as if we haven't talked all day. Again we laugh it off.

She's very beautiful, inside and out. She flows into the room and light flashes over her face. Wisps of blond hair brush to the side of her hazel eyes. "From death she casts her spell..." *Secret Garden* is an amazing musical. Perhaps we'll discuss its deeper meanings. If not, there's always *Hamlet*. I can always act like I know what's been going on in the play (I really need to try to stay awake more often). I shut and lock the door behind us. Wouldn't want anyone else walking in would we? Kaitlyn and I move towards the living room.

"Hey, you got two new fish!" she observes.

Two? Well, two is an even number.

I glare into the tank. I understand that untamed creatures will behave differently than those that are tamed, but for some reason I am unable to grasp how these two fish can just float at the bottom, not moving at all in my presence.

Wait! One just moved. The smaller of the two catfish darted behind a fake plant. I shift to the side of the tank and look inquisitively at the shadows lurking over the small fish. The plant's plastic leaves cast darkness over the whole fish, and yet somehow its eyes glow through the shadows, just as fog creeps slowly to the earth from above. This fish is the one. I can feel it. I feel it deep within me. Within each bone; each muscle; every drop of blood chills as I feel it. It is trapping. That glare seems to capture my mind in a way I cannot get out of. No matter how hard I try to free myself, I only find myself looking deeper and deeper into the clouds. Through the murkiness...

"Hello?" Kaitlyn calls to me.

I look up. She's sitting there smiling at me.

"What?" I ask.

"I'm sorry. Normally someone doesn't just stumble towards a fish aquarium, although it was graceful in its own way."

"Your point?"

"You just looked awkward, that's all," she laughs. "You let me in, and then five minutes later you were slowly crouching down and moving towards the fish aquarium."

"The glass was nice and cool on my face," I smile.

"Way to just zone out," she states.

I was unaware I did any of this. My body moved without control. But never mind now. Now Kaitlyn's here and we will have a fun time. We always do. We have ever since we met.

It was a crisp October night. Sister Hazel was to perform after an introduction by Jon McLaughlin (I still have the ticket stub).

As I sat in the smoky basement of some beaten down music store, more and more people trickled in from the steps of the nightlife above. I sat waiting, waiting for the music, waiting for that high from the lights and the sound, waiting for…her. She came down the steps.

Some man to my side said something about a missing band member. I did not concentrate on this. My mind was off. I didn't actually regain full consciousness until the first note was struck on the piano; then it was back to reality.

I lost her through the mass of people and the density of the smog; there was nothing I could do then. I decided to continue on.

The opening act took my heart away. I was off in a musical ecstasy when I noticed her standing next to me. She was tapping her hand against her thigh as she nodded her head from one side to the other. Left, right, left…tap, tap, tap. I was staring, and she knew.

"Hello."

We stood next to each other the rest of the night, not saying a single word.

After the concert we walked out the back doors, never leaving the others' side. We were both conscious of our bodies and we made sure not to touch the other unless bumped by a hurried patron ready to get to the nightlife.

A stream of cool air blew across my face as I walked out the doors. Sister Hazel's bus was parked right there. The bass-player stood outside as if nothing was different. A small crowed gathered. We walked to join and introduced ourselves.

"Kaitlyn."

Her name rolled off her lips as honey drips from a spoon.

We proceeded that night to go to the Village Inn together. She had some strange craving for pancakes. Ever since then, we met on Saturdays at the Village Inn. She got pancakes. I didn't eat. Instead, I just watched her. It's one of the traditions that have gotten us to where we stand today: right next to each other. Life-long friends. A love difficult to explain, but expressed in every "hello." Sure Village Inn faded long ago, but that really doesn't matter when you see someone most everyday (Kaitlyn still likes pancakes though).

Heading to the couch now, Kaitlyn follows right behind. We start to discuss the end of the world.

"What if the world was ending?" she asks.

"Like right now, in this very instant?"

"Would it matter if it was this very instant?" she asks.

"I don't know. I guess it depends on what you're asking about."

"What if the world was ending?" she repeats.

"What if it was? What do you want me to say?"

"I don't know. Say what you want. Like, what would you do?"

"I suppose I would sit down, because there's no point in standing up when the world is going to end. I would also smoke a cigar. Yeah. I think I would just sit down right here and smoke a cigar."

"How would you be able to get a cigar when the world is ending this very second?" she questions.

"Eh, good point. Well, why would we be talking if the world was ending this very second?"

"Because you like me," Kaitlyn throws it out smiling.

"Yeah...so? Your point?"

"Well you normally want to leave with the people you like," she states.

"Yeah. That's true. But would it really matter? I mean, the world is going to end any second, so what would be the deal in having life as you want it just as the world is ending? I'd rather have life as I want it while I can still live it that way."

"Good point," she mutters.

I win.

"I'd still talk to you though," I say.

"When do you think the will would end?" she asks.

"I don't know. It could be anytime I suppose."

"True," Kaitlyn says, "but why would it end when everyone expected it to end. Where's the fun in that?"

"You know, you're right there, Kaitlyn. The world probably is going to look down on us and think 'hmm…these people don't seem to expect me to end, so I will end.' Bam!" I say snapping.

I love sarcasm.

"Haha, very funny," Kaitlyn loves sarcasm, too. "So the world would end at a random time."

"Any time is random," I say.

"But I thought everything had a pattern," she inquires.

"Well, if everything has a pattern then it must be patternizized to randomness."

"*Patternizized*?" she says questioning my vocabulary.

"Look, I guess if the world was ending, it would probably end at 11:40 PM."

"Probably sometime in the winter too," she concludes.

We look at each other and smile. Glad that's over.

I turn to Kaitlyn and ask, "How would you feel if the world was over?"

"Well, there wouldn't be any feeling left," Kaitlyn points out.

Funny how life, or rather the absence of life, works out.

"True, but if your mind still went on?"

"I guess it would be sad," she says. "I know I would miss it."

We sit next to each other for five minutes and ponder our random conversation.

After sitting there, Kaitlyn hits me on my shoulder. Not this again. I look up and she's grinning wildly. She hops up off the couch and backs away holding the grin. After sitting on the couch weighing out whether or not it's worth it, I throw out a distracting remark.

"It sure is strange outside."

She turns her head to the window and I dart out of my seat to pursue her in our wild game. She sprints to the other side of the couch and I counter her.

I move toward her, the couch between us, and she gets me again. This time a slap to the face. She's still grinning like a madman. I back away.

With a quick glance to the floor, I run towards the couch and hurl myself over. Before she knows it, I'm on top of her, tickling like crazy. She crowds to the floor to cover her stomach up, but it is no use. Tears of laughter and that queer pain stream down her cheeks.

I look up at the aquarium, and the shadowed catfish is gaping wide-eyed at me. That's interesting.

As Kaitlyn calms down, she pulls something out of her pocket. It's a small clear bottle filled with a clear liquid.

The first time I ever tasted alcohol was at a party. No it was not with a bunch of teenage children running around in ignorance doing foolish acts (I went to one of these once and found it too unpleasant for my pleasure, however it was quite fun to mess with people).

My first drink occurred with adults. Surely I was no more than ten years of age. I coughed. I went to some holiday party with my parents. It was for my dad's work, or maybe it was for my mom's. There were some faces I recognized from pictures, but most of the people were basically wearing a mask.

It was not the will of another the first time I touched the stuff. It was my own choice. Unfortunately (or fortunately), I soon came to realize the power of the drink. This was before I even touched it.

While milling around the party, listening in on various conversations about politics, religion, and the weather, I spotted a hand leave a cup on a wooden counter. My eyes glanced at the cup and then around the room.

I stayed in my spot to see if anyone was coming to pick it back up. I didn't know what was in the cup, but I knew it must have been something good, because all of the adults were holding these cups. These simple yellow plastic cups with little indentions on the side, just like the one on the counter, held a whole new world inside.

After holding my ground, I couldn't resist anymore. I slowly sidestepped toward the drink, keeping my eyes around the room. No one was watching.

Just then, a man with a big white beard saw me and gave me a questioning glance. I darted off into another room.

I planted myself on the wall in a dark corner, so the world couldn't see me. I had to have what was in that cup. No matter what it would take. By the end of the night, that cup would be mine.

After about five minutes, I sat down in my corner. What if the cup was not there when I returned? What if my dreams were to be smashed? When would the next party be? What if the bearded man told them something? Would my parents ever let me come to another party like this?

There was too much to lose, but then again, there was much to gain. My desires sank over me like the onset of a thunderstorm. After thirty minutes, the rain overtook my mind.

I stood. As if in a trance, I moved toward the room with the wooden counter, with the cup. There was someone in the way, but that would not stop me. I walked straight toward the counter, unsure if the cup was there.

The person moved. The cup was there. I reached my hand out and took the cup in my grip. The whole room zoomed in on me, but I did not care. As I raised the cup, the man with the white beard let out a chuckle. It was too late to turn back.

I took the cup to my mouth and touched the rim to my lips. I threw the cup back like I had seen the adults do with the miniature glasses, just as everyone turned to look. The small amount of liquid trickled down my throat. It burned. I tried to control myself, but I couldn't suppress the urge to cough. As I let out the little tickle in my throat, the room erupted into laughter.

My head began to spin as I saw my dad emerge from the crowd. My dad didn't seem to mind in front of the other adults, but then he took me out back.

There was an old wooden deck out back, one that gives off splinters with even the slightest touch. My dad took me to this and stopped at the top of the stairs.

"I don't have a coat on, Dad!"

He laughed and then straightened out. He led me down the stairs, out of the view of the party. His face turned serious.

"Stay here," he commanded.

My dad went inside. My heart pounded in anticipation. When he came back out, he had two bottles and a yellow, plastic cup. Perhaps he is going to treat me as a man.

He poured a cup a quarter full with some brownish liquid, shoved it into my hands, and told me to drink.

"It'll warm me up, right?"

My dad turned away from my comment.

As I slowly sipped the cup, my dad turned and looked at me, his face like a stone.

"Drink like a man."

I tilted the cup up a little higher.

"Drink like a man, son!"

A little poured out the side of my lip. My dad grabbed the cup and filled it back up, this time full to the top of the rim.

"Drink."

I relentlessly took the cup from my dad. A tear formed in my eyes.

"Wipe those tears away and drink like a man."

I put the cup to my mouth and began to drink slowly. The world began to spin worse than ever before.

"Drink it like a man!"

I coughed as the liquid clogged my throat.

"Drink it like a goddamn man!"

I closed my mouth, and the liquid poured out over my face. I turned to the side and hurled out my desire, or so my dad thought. He was satisfied; I was sick.

Kaitlyn flashes a smile. I never can stop looking at her when she smiles. This only makes her smile more.

And as her grin grows and my eyes widen, she unscrews the bottle.

It's not the first time we've drank together, just never alone. There have been parties, there are always parties, but this is different. It is like she is asking me to break that social barrier and change how we feel about our friendship. I don't quite know what she wants out of this. My face shows it.

"It'll be fun," she offers to dampen my puzzled look.

After thinking for a second, I decide, "Why not?"

I walk to the cupboard and pull out two small glasses.

Did she mean for us both to drink the entire bottle? I've never had that much since my dad forced the alcohol down my throat. I'm sure I could handle it.

Nevertheless, she opens the bottle and pours us each a little, straight up. Just the way I remember it. It's how I've grown to like it, and she knows that.

One drink won't do any harm. Besides, she'll just stay over tonight, so there's no worry of her driving off. Just in case, I take her keys when she's not looking.

She smiles at me. I look hard at her. We raise our glasses and toast.

"To memories!" she says.

"To memories."

The liquid trickles down my throat. I cough a little. She giggles as she drinks a cup of water. At least I don't need the water.

We sit there for a little bit and let the drink take hold. I let out a sigh, and she leans in to kiss me. I back away with a nervous hesitation.

What is she trying to do? Is this what she wanted to do this for? Surely she knows it wouldn't take alcohol to do that.

I laugh it off and change the subject.

"Do you know anything about wood?" I ask honestly.

What a boring subject. As we sit there and ramble off all the different types of wood we can think of, the clock ticks away.

"Cedar, maple, oak..."

I glance at the bottom fish aquarium and notice a body floating at the top. It's one of my albino catfish.

"Ash, birch, hickory..."

The sun sets through a window to the outside world.

"Elm, mahogany, rosewood..."

Kaitlyn begins to pour another drink.

I've always seemed to like trees. I'm not really sure where it comes from. They're comforting in me. People make jokes of tree-huggers. I am literally one of these.

My dad used to drive the family to a Christmas tree farm. My mom would sit in the shotgun seat, while my brother and I shared the back. We drove an old beat-up blue van. It had one door for the back seats on the left side. I always preferred sitting on the left. I liked to be able to get out as quickly as I could. My brother didn't mind. His side didn't have a hole in the seat.

As we pulled into the tree farm, my mom popped out the Christmas tape we had been listening to. None of us could really sing, but that never stopped us from hurting our throats. My mom was the worst.

One time, after driving around looking for a gas station, my mom turned to my brother and me and said in a deep raspy voice that was barely audible, "Why haven't you been answering me?"

We just stared blankly into her eyes, wondering if she was serious. Apparently she had been asking questions about the past school semester.

After just sitting there blankly, she tried to yell at us. This only resulted in a comical display much like the pope trying to sing a rock song. My dad grinned, but this was quickly shot down with a glance from my mother.

None of us really minded occurrences like these. We knew she meant well (even if she did sound like a chain-smoker).

I remember smoke coming from a fire in the middle of the tree farm. The fire was small, but the warmth stretched for miles. It seemed to call the community around its shifting chimney of smoke.

We always rushed right out of the van and straight to the fire. I was the first out, but my brother, being older and stronger, always beat me there. We all huddled around the fire and sipped on complimentary apple cider. My tongue was burned easily; I regretfully welcomed the pain. It would be a memory imprinted on my tongue for weeks to come.

It was a wonderful time. My dad went out to the van to get an axe. It was a rather small axe, but he still looked like Paul Bunyan as he carried his axe to us.

Picking out the tree was a rather random process. My brother and I each stood next to a tree we saw as the most appropriate. Then my dad told us to pick a number.

"Two," my brother said.

"One," I stated proudly, even if the more logical choice was three.

It really didn't matter though -- they always let me win this skillful game. My dad turned to my mom, and she looked back, forgetting what she was supposed to do.

"Oh! 'One' it is. You win this year!" She finally remembered her line of the time-rehearsed script.

Now that I come to think of it, I can't remember ever losing.

"Stand back son, this could be dangerous," dad said in that deep, Paul Bunyan voice.

I moved to the side as he moved toward the tree. Wiping the axe-blade once with his shirt, he raised the axe into the air and sliced it quickly to the tree, but he stopped a few inches before the trunk. He repeated this action several times to "warm up" as he put it.

Finally coming to one with the environment, my dad was ready to commence the process. He swung the axe back and forth in a flurry of passion, always hitting his mark. After about five minutes, he invited my brother and me over to stand next to him.

"Go to work!" he exclaimed.

My brother and I each took turns throwing our bodies against the tree. I think my parents got quite an enjoyment out of the tree slinging me back into the ground each time I ran and jumped against it. After about three hard pushes from my brother, we all yelled "timber!" and watched as the tree crackled to the ground. We now had a tree to provide us a holiday filled with memories (and if my brother and I were lucky, maybe a little wine as well).

Ever look at the wood of a desk? It's really quite interesting. I mean inside of a tree there are all the patterns that we never see, rings and what not. And then there's a desk. The wood is just kind of spread out. Cut to the needed shape and spread out like butter. Makes you take a different look at a tree.

I'm sifting through my desk. It's something I haven't done in quite a while. As a matter of fact, make that about five years or more. It's hilarious what you find. It's like going through old boxes with memories packed tightly inside.

Mickey Bahr

After sifting through some scattered papers, I sight some familiar shapes. I love old school assignments. They always made us write about the most ridiculous things. We wrote about the past, our past. No one wants to hear about your past, let alone a fieldtrip you took in fifth grade. Who wants to read something that takes more energy to think about than pleasure received? Here's one of my papers. It's from fifth grade, about a fieldtrip I took.

At 7:00 A.M. the bus left for Agrirama in Tifton, GA. It took us two hours to get there. At 8:00 we ate breakfast. I had a bagle and some grapes. I sat in the back with Marlen. When we finaly got to Agrirama it was 9:00. We went to a house to put on suspenders and skirts. The boys wore suspenders and the girls wore skirts. After we were suited up, we went to work. I was a farmer along with Josh, Daniel, Danny, Franz, and Stevan. The first thing we did was milk the cow and scoop biskits (poop). Milking the cow felt weaird, but was fun. Everytime you squized one of the utters milk would squirt out. Sometimes, I missed the pale! When we got to scoop biskits, the first thing you had to do was rake it in to a pile. Next, you take a shuvel and rake all the biskits into it. Lastly, you put all the biskits into a weel baral and take it away. Next Daniel, Danny, and I got to cut wood. You had to use this huge saw with two handles and work fast. While the other three boys took over, we got to draw water from a well. The well was 20 to 30 feet deep! We gave the water to the mules. Then it was lunch time! We all got to ride in a buggie that we set up. When we arived at the house we had to wash out hands. Then we sat down to eat. There was chicken noodle woup, green beans, cream corn, and corn bread. When you ate, you could only have one hand on the table. You also had to pass the food in a circle. When we were done with the fabulus meal, it was time for school. The boys sat on one side and the girls on the other. They didn't have erasers back then so you had to write extreamly careful if you had paper. Some schools didn't have paper because it was so much money. We also used a slate board to do a math paper on. When it was time to read, row one stool up and went to a bench in front of the desk. We read some rules from a book. I learnd that once you are done reading eight books, you can be a teacher. Also there are only 8 grades! When school was over we all boarded the bus for a long trip home. Agrirama was a fun trip to go on and I hope I can do it again some day!

Great story huh? I remember that day. It was a good day. I actually do wish I could go back now.

Here's another one. I think it's from the seventh grade. Oh yeah, we were told to use our imaginations and write about a virtue that would take a lot in life to truly grasp the significance of.

The End of the World

It all started on a cool misty day in October. The German general came through the loud doors of the American naval base. "Give us your land or let this be World War 9!" he said.

The American general said, "This will be a nuclear war."

The Germans left and the war began! There were bombs everywhere, killing everyone except three boys, because they were hiding in an old mine shaft. They came out when they heard no sound. Tony said, "What happened?"

"I have no clue," said Josh.

"Do you think anyone else is alive?" asked Daniel.

"I don't know," the other two boys said at the same time. The world was still green with air and water! "We must have been in that mine shaft for a long time because everything grew back," said Daniel.

"No, I heard about a new bomb they made that only kills people if the shock wave can get to them," said Tony.

"I think you're right because all the buildings are still here," said Josh. They all started to go explore. They explored for two days and ate what was in the mall.

Then on the third day Tony said, "Lets make some robots!" They all started to get supplies from car stores. In 30 days they had built 15 robots! Josh, Tony, and Daniel got everything they wanted because the robots did all the work.

One hot summer day Tony said, "I kind of miss my family." "Me too," said Josh.

Daniel said, "Lets make a time machine from our creations." They all agreed to build a time machine and they got started. When they were finished, they all sat admiring their work of art. The time machine looked a little awkward, but they thought it would do.

After they got in the time machine, Tony said, "Are you sure it will work?"

"I hope so," Josh said.

Daniel started pressing all the buttons and said, "Here we go!" They all felt a shock and suddenly they were all right there! Right in front of the naval base just as a German general walked in. They got out and ran as quickly as they could to the big doors of the naval base. They rushed in to tell them not to have the war.

As soon as they were in, two guards told them to leave. Tony, Daniel, and Josh pushed past them. When they were finally into the main room. They told their story. No one believed them. They "dragged" everyone outside to see the time machine. The American general turned on the power switch and it worked. Everyone agreed not to have the war and the three boys were escorted home.

When they got home they hugged there mom and dad. They ate a nice chicken dinner and went up to bed. They swore not to tell anyone about the end of the world.

The next morning Tony got up early and turned on the news, "Japan has declared war on Asia," the news man said.

"No", Tony said, "not again!"

At least the grammar and spelling improved a little. Still no concept of world relations, but it's true. It really is true. It would take someone a lot in life to grasp the significance of family.

To be completely honest, I always felt a sort of mythical glow every time I was in a church. Catholic churches were the best to bring about that feeling of Roman rule. Must have been the alter.

I could only imagine alters through history. I never really understood what they were for. Some have you gathering around the alter. Others have you separated from the alter, like the alter is some sort of holy station that only the highest ranking members can take part in. And then there's my favorite: the sacrificial alter. I don't know why, but for some reason people don't like to be up next to that alter.

The Aztecs used those things. I had a friend in elementary school; his name was Franz. He was a transfer student from Mexico. Each day he would bring in different pictures of life in his part of the world. I could see why people would want to live there and get away.

Besides the water, Mexico didn't look that bad. There was something that brought the pictures alive. Not like the Aboriginal belief of the photograph stealing your soul (which would explain a lot of famous people, movie stars, Hitler), there was something in his voice.

Franz had a story to tell with each picture. It was he that brought the pictures to life.

"Ah! Luk hare. Deh es mi huse!" Franz said in his native dialect, a mix of Spanish and Aztec.

He told us of how his house was built on ancient burial ground. Immediately everyone could feel the spirits coming up from underneath them. He continued on, and pretty soon you were living his life in the dry land.

So there I was with my brother, digging up skulls in Mexico. The skulls were divided into two teams, and they were kicked at each other to see whose side had the thicker heads. You could always tell a good skull by the size of the jaw. If the jaw was small, they had talked it away while alive, thus giving you a bad skull. A big jaw meant a strong skull. Of course this had been tested over and over ten fold, as this game was passed on through many generations.

Selecting the skulls was the hard part. It was kind of like a jury selection. You had to make sacrifices sometimes in hopes of getting what you needed.

Once selecting was done, my brother and I would take places opposite of each other and kick the skulls at each other's side. It was a unique skill that developed over many games played.

Unfortunately time ran out as the teacher called roll, and we began our day of normal acting. The teacher acted like she cared about our future, and we acted like we were listening. It's an arrangement that goes on for years.

Days are wasted. Nights are the only time to truly accomplish anything. In the passing of days, youth is lost. In the passing of nights, youth is shown for what it really is: a fleeting dream some had.

Man, it's already November, November 24th. It's been a long, long year. It's funny how we measure time. Some measure it in days. Some live by the minute. Some adjust their life to their job or to school. Whatever, it doesn't really matter. It's all relative, right?

I should get out. Or should I stay in? Why not a little bit of both? And so I walk to the pantry and stare at the options of food. I close the door. Open. Close. Open.

Light on. Light off. Close. I check the fridge. Open. Close. Nothing. Absolutely nothing.

Maybe there is something. I think I still have a little left. Just a little, but it'd be enough. I reach up to the top drawer and open. Yes! There is some. Just a little. Just enough.

I pull down the dusty bottle of Brandy and twist the top off. Just a little. Just enough. I take a swig. It burns. I cough, just a little. The drink was perfect. Just enough.

I sit down on the couch. What else do I have to do? I guess I could go somewhere, but where? Maybe just a little drive. That might be nice.

I grab my keys, go to the garage, and turn the car on. It sounds the same as last time. I open the garage door and head on out. I'll just drive around the block a little.

I drive down the road, going relatively slow. It's a nice relaxed pace, maybe a pace an elder person would drive. I can see why they drive like that. It's so much nicer to slow down a little bit and just enjoy life a little more. There's an elderly man walking on the sidewalk.

Suddenly time lurches to a hold. He seems lonely. Should I talk to him? He seems like a nice man. I wonder what his story is. I wonder what he sounds like. He's really frail; looks like he could use some food, that's for sure, but maybe that's not what he needs or wants.

There is this look on his face. His eyes are sad, but his mouth is wrinkled to cover up any sign of emotion. What happened to him?

Our eyes connect for one single tenth of a second. And there I was, walking. There's one old man, but there's no younger man. I have disappeared, yet I am still present. The old man is sad, but he's afraid to show it. He loved once, but it was taken from him. He had a home once, but he had to leave it. He ate once, but then he lost his apatite. He lived once, but then he lost all will.

I look down at my feet. Suddenly the penny loafers from the 1930s don't seem so strange. They are not my own, yet I feel comfort. At least a little comfort. Just enough.

Then I am down the road, past the aged man, past the cracks in the sidewalk. There's a car in front of me now, and there's a car in front of it. A pattern begins to form. Why does this happen? I just wanted a nice slow pace, not a complete stop. Who is causing them to slow? I'll take care of the problem. Somehow I'll do something.

We're moving, just a little. Just enough. There are lights flashing. There's a car. For some reason it doesn't look like it should. Maybe it's the inversion of direction. Maybe it's the steam forming off a recently smothered fire. Stupid car accidents. Stupid cars. God it just makes me so angry. Why would anyone get behind the wheel of the car if they know they might not make it? There's a blanket sitting on the side of the road. Under the blanket, there's a body. I can see its shape just a little. Just enough.

The last time I viewed a dead body, even partially, was of my great-grandfather. He lived to the ripe young age of 97. He was the only grandparent I had surviving, and boy was he a great one! I really could not have asked for anything better.

He died right in front of my face.

But besides that, he really was a pretty interesting man. He always had a new story, and if he had forgotten the ones told in the past, he just rewound a little and told one again. I was never really bothered. Then again, being only nine gives very little opportunity for true understanding of wisdom.

He was the last elder in my family to live. He had been through quite a lot. His wife died extremely early in life (after of course all the children were born). He raised that family single handedly, literally single handedly. He lost one of his arms while serving in the military. It wasn't even wartime, but that doesn't mean a cable can't break on a ship and snap a man's arm off. That might have been one of my favorite stories. He didn't even cry. I guess it's hard when you black out.

And so after raising his kids to see them have kids, they all just kind of died off one by one until he was the only one left. It's not right for the kids to die before their parents, but it still happens. Over time he just had to grow old with his feelings of loneliness, which is expected.

His stories came from around the world. After retiring from the military with all the benefits that come with losing an arm, he had to get a job to raise the kids.

So he worked in some shop selling shoes and saved up for the future. After investing his money in the right areas (something called Wal-Mart) he decided to take some time for himself and see the world he had missed over the years. Each time he returned, he stopped around to see each of his remaining family members.

And so in stopping by after visiting the upper portions of Russia (and freezing his ass off), my great-grandpa started complaining of headaches. He started to say that it's just his body adjusting to the change from the ultra cold climate. I guess headaches like that come with change. It could be stress; it could be a busted blood vessel in the brain, who knows?

Anyways, he left for one year and ran around China for a little while. When he came back from spreading his influence over the communist block, he decided to see us first. He didn't have an address or a phone, he just showed up whenever he felt like. Over the years we learned to expect him whenever. He was an old man in his nineties, but he got around like a fifty-year-old on steroids (minus the negative effects). It was quite a sight to see the great G drive up in some hot-rod rental car on the weekend.

So this one weekend when he returned from China, he pulled up and knocked on the door. I was the only one home at the time. I think my brother had some engagement with the Boy Scouts or something. I was cleaning up when I answered the door, and there stood the man of many years. He was styling a newly grown facial animal-fur that really needed to be shaved, and he hunched over like he never had before.

We said our hellos, but this time his hello was said with a suppressing pain. He came in and asked if he could lie down for a little bit; didn't even inquire as to the location of the rest of his remaining family. I led him to his normal room (my room, then I would have to sleep with my brother, get pushed off the bed, and end up on the floor, blanket-less).

After he sat there on the bed for a little bit, just staring at the floor, he looked up at me and mumbled a little something.

"What was that?" I asked him.

He sighed and just said, "Kid, it hurts too much to be alone. You should be with your family."

"I know, but it's fine. Besides, I can't 'cause they're at something for my brother," I replied.

"You'll learn kid. Someday you'll understand."

And with that he just smiled at me, rolled his eyes up, and dropped back on the bed right there. My bed, his death.

My family was left with mixed feelings after his passing. There was a release from the constant stress of worrying when it, the day, his death would come; no more would he visit. There was also a great sense of loss and loneliness in that there was no one left to watch over us; no more would he visit.

My bed, his death. I guess it had to happen, but it still doesn't feel right to sleep there at night.

My head hurts. There's a throbbing pain in my arm. I open my eyes.

Once again, I am staring at the forest on the floor. I'm lying over my arm that's losing circulation. I roll over and hit my head on something. My head throbs with a slow pulse.

It's not a migraine. I've never awakened with a migraine. They usually develop throughout the day and hit me hard just as I sit down to relax at night. But I only get those once or twice a year.

This is different. Everything just feels clammy. I try to swallow, but there's no moisture in my throat. I cough.

I push my hand against my right eye, where it hurts the most. The pain moves to the left side of my head. Through my left eye I see what I had hit my head on.

I must have fallen asleep on the carpet right in front of the fish aquariums. The water still waves back and forth in the bottom tank. That one catfish is still there; the beast.

"Kaitlyn?"

There's no reply.

"Kaitlyn, are you here?"

Still no reply.

I stand up very slowly. Too quickly. The blood rushes to my head. Slowly everything goes black.

I open my eyes again and I'm back on the floor. I just need to take a shower, and then I'll feel better.

I stand up again, this time without any lightheadedness. I take one step and my knee buckles under. My leg must have fallen asleep. I stumble and bang against the wall. A picture frame falls.

There's a shatter. It's a picture of my parents standing over the Grand Canyon. There's a tear now right down the middle of the canyon. That was one of my favorite pictures.

I remember that trip like it was yesterday. It might be a little bit of a dream mixed up in there, but what's the difference when it comes to memories? I've only had a problem with taking on dreams as reality once in my life, and it was when I was flat out called out on a lie.

"What! You've never jumped out of an airplane while being shot at!"

"Yeah...I guess that is a little crazy, but it seemed so real. Must have been a dream."

And life moved on. Who doesn't get a little confused every once in a while? You wake up right after a dream and feel the feelings of the dream in reality. You feel good (if it was a good dream), or you feel bad (if it was obviously and respectively a bad dream). Nevertheless, it's hard to tell what reality is sometime. Greatest quote in the world:

"'Life as it is.' I have lived for over forty years and I've seen 'life as it is'. Pain. Misery. Cruelty beyond belief. I've heard all the voices of God's noblest creature -- moans from bundles of filth in the street. I've been a soldier and a slave. I've seen my comrades fall in battle or die more slowly under the lash in Africa. I've held them at the last moment. These were men who saw 'life as it is,' but they died despairing. No glory. No bray of last words. Only their eyes, filled with confusion, questioning, 'Why?' I do not think they were asking why they were dying, but why they had ever lived. When life itself seems lunatic, who knows where madness lies? Perhaps to be too practical is madness. To surrender dreams, this may be madness. To seek treasure where there is only trash. Too much sanity may be madness. But maddest of all -- to see life as it is, and not as it should be!"

Now that right there is just beautiful. Peter O'Toole from Man of La Mancha (Miguel de Cervantes' Don Quixote, which was originally in Spanish and really loses its power when translated to English, as so many foreign pieces do. I guess Peter's accent helps).

Dream: Freud wrote of those things. They are supposed to shed light on our lives. I guess they could, but the entire connection would be extremely irrelevant to what you do with your life, which is why sometimes I just have to throw the books down.

Dreams. Some people believe these are the ties to an alternant reality. These are obviously some people who hang around too much at rock concerts and have exposure to...outside influences. There's only one reality, and that's the one we make, the one we believe.

Dreams. I'll stick to "life as it is" for this. I tried to have that "life as it should be," but sometimes we aren't given a choice as to what we can do with our lives. How much control do we really have. If it was up to me, I'd like to be in the clouds above and strike people with bolts of lightning, but then again, we can't all play God (only those with a lot of money in today's world).

Still, those times when I wake up, and I don't really know if I'm awake yet or if I'm still asleep and just having one of those double dreams, I tend to not worry about the confusion of questioning which reality I'm in, and just go with what I remember.

So back to the Grand Canyon. Here's what I remember of that day. I was somewhere around nine years old, making my dad about 45, my mom about...and you thought I'd say my mother's age. One thing I learned young is to let a woman keep her age and her weight to herself (although it's always fun to joke with. "Hey mom! How old are you, 46?" and she'd say, "Hell no! What are you trying to pull?" and then you just sit there and smile. Oh, good times). And my brother would have been somewhere around...I don't know. He was older than I was.

I remember another uncle with us. That would've been one of my dad's brothers. We'll call him Jack. So we're all at the Grand Canyon (it truly is a beautiful place). I mean where else does the cold of night and the warmth of day keep you thirsty all the time? Besides the lack of hydration we failed to plan for, there was a constancy of energy in the group that I fail to hold in my younger years (I was lazy, I admit it). Everyone was eagerly hiking and walking and all those fun and dandy outdoor activities you can image a family doing in the Grand Canyon, when my dad and his brother decided to go for a race.

"Well Jack, you think you still have what it takes to beat your younger brother? Looks to me like the grays in your hair are starting to catch up to you," my dad grinned.

"You think you can beat me? Ha! I still have the record in this family don't I? It's on!"

They broke off with my mother screaming in sobs for them to be careful.

They ran off into the distance while I pattered behind to keep up, which somehow I actually accomplished. Running, running, running, all the way to a cliff and a drop into the great canyon below. And for some reason, they just ran straight to the edge and stopped just inches from the mile-high drop. My mom caught up and calmly took the camera out and took a picture (the one that was up on the wall), and then my dad and uncle decided to climb down, which they did. The rest of us jumped down to them and then went on with our merely day.

There's another version with something like a volcano erupting and burning everyone alive, but I think that was our trip to Hawaii, and no one survived that dream. We don't have any pictures from that.

Ah, my dad was right. Tomorrow is another day. He always told me that, but I never really got it, but I get it now. Just woke up and this day, yesterday's tomorrow, is different from yesterday.

I'm in my nice room. My eyes feel refreshed -- none of that goopy stuff in them. My mouth is nice and ripe. I'll have to brush later. But that's not going to stop anything. It's another day.

So I flip my bedside light on, and suddenly the walls flash shades of red. There is blood splattered all over the walls. I look around and see the swishes and swoops of a fight. But whose blood is it?

I look down at my stomach, and see that it is my own. I have been cut across the chest and belly, and the crimson spirits are flowing from the crevices.

Up again. I hate those double dreams, the ones where you dream something, then you dream about waking up from that dream and dream something else, they get me every time. But again, it's a new day. So there's a little goop in my eyes. Oh well, it happens. What time is it? Six o'clock in the morning! I'm never up naturally at six. Surely I'm tired, but I don't feel tired. If my body is playing tricks on me, I swear it's going to regret it. I just know how it's going to work. I'll wake up for a little bit, and then in three hours or so I'll barely be able to keep my eyes open. Whatever, maybe I have gotten enough sleep. Let's see. Slept some during the day, and then fell asleep around nine last night. Well that isn't too bad. Why not wake up?

What to do, what to do?

"Mom! Dad!"

No answer. There's no one here. Guess I'm on my own. It's better that way. Being alone every so often. Now I can do exactly whatever it is that I feel like doing.

So what do I feel like doing? What great thing can I accomplish today? Where shall I lay my influence?

I flip the television on and lay down on the couch. Hmm…I don't like that channel, that doesn't look good, commercial, commercial, commercial, a show, but I don't like that show, another commercial, more crap, there! There's something. Oh, it's just a soap opera. More crap, crap, crap, crap! Dang. There's nothing on.

I hate it when this happens, I mean. It seems to happen all the time. The only thing I can do is turn the television off and continue on with my dull life, or I can turn it to some random channel and watch the dullness into my life. It's better to have dullness shoved into your life than to just sit in dullness, so I press the remote until two random numbers appear. 57. That's nice. The History Channel. But of course there's only some dullness of a commercial on. Maybe history can be relied on for something. I'll just watch this for a little while. Maybe I'll just close my eyes a little bit.

Up again.

"You're not dreaming."

There. I'm awake for sure this time. I always say that whenever I'm unsure. Never could I have the logic to say that in a dream. One of these days it'll probably bite me in the butt though.

Still commercials. What was I thinking? Well, it's only been an hour. I'll just shut it off and find something else to -- hmm, what's this commercial?

"If you or a loved one has experienced a wrongful death, call the law offices of…"

Ha! I can see it now:

"Hi, yes, I just died, and I think it was someone else fault. Do you think you could sue them for me? Thanks!"

That's just ridicules. Whatever, people don't think these days anyway. They just say what would be incorrect because of some political reason. It's what falls within the boundaries of the law. This is exactly why I stay out of that mess. If I got in it, I know I would waste my life trying to take everything apart, so it could be built up like never before. But I would have to be dictator for something like that, another thing that's not accepted. Oh well, I'll just stick to my normal life, in this normal house, in this normal town.

There was one point in my life when I wanted to die a very painful death. Normally, it's expected this would be a result of some depression, as this seems only something someone with a lot of pain in their life would wish upon themselves. To me it seems if you had a lot of pain in your life, you'd want to die without pain. It makes more sense to balance things out. But I was not depressed. Not at all.

I had it all mapped out, in a way. It seemed to change every time someone asked me how I wanted to die.

"How would you like to die?" someone would ask, just after saying their wishes for a peaceful death.

They expected the same answer. I never did see why they would ask me then.

"Well, I've always wanted to die a very painful death. I know it sounds strange, but I have a logical explanation for it."

After getting over the normal shock of this unexpected answer, they always let me continue. It ended up making sense to many of them.

"You know how you have pain in life. I mean, everyone has some sort of physical pain in their life; it's just natural. If someone couldn't feel pain, think about how much trouble they would have in life. I don't know how much I learned from the first temptation of touching the hot stove, but I do know that it hurt, and immediately afterwards, I put my finger in ice-water. Just right there, I learned something that would change me for the rest of my life. And in a way, pain defines us as individual. Every scar has a story, a lesson learned. But this aside, we all have pain in our life, and no matter how you look at it, pain is good in some way. It makes us stronger; it helps us to survive. It truly is something great. My God, pain is good!"

At this, their eyes always opened wide. They sucked it all up right into their head. It was like melting butter on bread in a microwave, two minutes on high power.

"Yes, that's right, pain is good. It is. I have had pain in my life, lots of it, both physical and mental pain. We all have it. To me, I would like to think that death brings something else than pain in life. I like to think of an afterlife after life, because it's pleasing to my mind and spirit. I like to think that afterlife is full of pleasure in many ways. I mean, we all want to have eternal happiness. Wouldn't that be wonderful?"

They nod their heads.

"Imagine a life where you've had pain. Imagine never having to deal with it again. Imagine that cloud where you are eternally happy. I hope to get there some day. And when I get there, I don't want to look back and think that I hadn't conquered anything in my life. Pain for me is something to get over. Isn't that what it's there for? To get over in one way or another? It is. Every cut and scrape as a child is eventually overcome; you stop crying in time. Maybe it takes three hours, but the pain eventually goes away. We get over pain. And for this, I want to die a painful death."

They still don't understand.

"Look: pain is a final push. It's a final hurrah to go out with. It's exciting. It's adventurous. It's how I want to die."

"Wow," they say, "but how?"

"What do you mean how? I just spent five minutes of straight explanation!"

"No, how would you want to die?"

"Oh," I finally got that they didn't want an explanation.

They sit there looking, waiting as I acted like I was thinking up something extreme, when the whole time I had known what I was going to say.

"Ok. Here: I'd want my body to be tingling with pain all over, so put me on top of a cliff. Pour gasoline on me, and then stab me a million times with a fork or something small like that. Light a match and throw it on me as you push me over the cliff. On the way down, my body will catch fire all over, and just before I would die from the fire, I would land in water. As the steam comes off the water, sharks would begin to circle. The biggest of them all would come up and swallow me whole, well at least after taking a couple chews. At this time, I would explode into a million pieces from the timed explosives placed in my stomach. Bam! And then eternal peace."

"Wow, that's interesting, weird but interesting," they always said and walked away.

I understand why now. I was young and immature. Even if the thought had logic behind it, it was just immoral and sickening. However, I'm yet to hear of a more painful death.

I guess that's how life goes. We have these ideas that seem to make sense, but it only takes time until we finally realize the truth. When we can look back onto it and think, why would I ever think something like that? But it's understandable, I mean, I was only like fifteen or sixteen.

There was only one person that understood this thought, and for this I placed her in my death fantasy. She didn't really like it.

In my dream, she didn't die. I did though, and this is what she didn't like. Even though it was the most romantic, action-filled ending to my life I could imagine, she didn't like it. I did though.

We would both be in a hut, a pueblo house on top of a grass hill. Just after professing my love for her, we could truly understand everything in our lives, and we would be happy. At this, I would need to go. I would turn to her, and through the silence of the breeze blowing through the open windows, we would look at each other, and she would understand. It was time for me to die. Everything in our lives was settled. I would put on my sunglasses and step out of the door. A black van would drive up and three men would get out. A gun would appear in my hand. I would walk towards them without fear. They would pull out there guns. One would fire and hit me in the shoulder. I would continue on. I had a mission. I would raise my gun, and with the thought of my love in the protection of heart and hut, I would fire my gun, killing two of the three men. The third would reach for a button in the van. I would run to stop him, only to end up next to the van staring at my love through a window as the van exploded, enveloping me in its flames.

She didn't understand why I had to die, but to me it all made sense. One of those thoughts you look back on and don't understand. I could've lived without trouble in the story, but for some reason I had to die at the time I created the imagination.

This always reminds me a lot of little kids, in a way myself. I often laugh at the thought, but it's real. Look at any child in that state when they can only grasp those simple thoughts. Where you can tell them something is hot, but they still have to touch it and burn themselves before fully understanding the concept of "hot." I think we never truly lose that need of experience to ultimately grasp ideas. It leads many to their final experience and then bam! Death.

There's nothing wrong with death. For a while, I had a hard time understanding this concept, but I came to understand that we all must die sometime. Oh well, there's nothing to be done about that. It's an idea that is grasped with experience. It's an idea that is grasped with time and reflection. It's an idea that is grasped when your parents die.

PART II

It was in November. November 24th was the day I received a phone call while I was home alone. God, the day is such a blur I can't really recall the important facts of the day. I know the news I received. I know what had happened. I remember what I was wearing. I remember the brand of toothpaste I had used when I woke up in the morning. I remember these simple, non-important frivolities, but I can't recall anything worth remembering.

It's been stated in the sciences that memory works best under the influence of stress and pressure. It's because of this that we are able to remember the most horrific events in our life. The most common example that I can think up is the events of September 11th. I remember where I was, what I was doing, and what I did for the rest of the day.

I was still in middle school, in eighth grade. It was D period, but it was the first period of the morning. We had this strange rotation of classes throughout the school year. Nevertheless, D period was first period this time of year. The day began as any other day, as I cannot remember coming to school that day or walking into the classroom. But I do remember sitting down. The sound of the television was droned out in the background by the talking of a hormonal group of becoming teenagers. But then there was that one picture that caught my eye.

As the images flashed across the screen, they were encoded into my brain, never to be let out. I remember what it looked like with both buildings standing, because I had been up in the towers. I remember what it looked like with one building leaking out the flames while the other still stood strong. I remember the crushing of freedom as the second plane hit the remaining building. I remember thinking, "what is going on?" I remember the words "terrorist" and "hijacking" flashing across the bottom of the screen. I remember the silence of the class as we all sat in awe. I remember the falling of the first pillar of dreams. I remember the smashing of the remaining grasps of hope. I remember my teacher, Mr. Harm, whispering the words, "God help us…"

And this was how I felt as I let the phone hang from its cord. I do not remember who called me, and it was not until later that I learned how they had died. I simply remember a strange voice on the other end stating with solemnity, "Your parents have passed."

And as these few words echoed in my head, and as the phone swung back and forth with liberty, I remember thinking, "God help us. No, God help me." And it was with these words that my eyes were truly opened for the first time.

You think you know the world. You think you know what it's like to truly live. You say that life isn't fair and that bad things are bound to happen. You say all this, but it's never truly grasped. You think you know life, but you don't -- not until the dreams and hopes come crashing down, leaving nothing but a barren, dusty world underneath.

I hate nights like this. Something creepy always happens. I sit here acting all normal like, just reading or watching or doing something of no importance, and then it just happens. Just like that. Again, like that. That period is about the amount of time it takes to have that feeling come over. Sure it's all relative, but relatives are usually predictable. This is not. Not at all.

I'm being watched. I know I am. It's the way the night is. It's the sounds I hear. It's the way I feel. Everything is just too perfect. It's calm outside, no storms. It's always better when there's at least a little rain. At least that gives some dulling to the sounds creaking throughout the house, not to mention a reason for the power to go out, which it just did. Damn it. I hate things like this.

There's that noise again. And again. It's coming from above, in the attic. Right by the vent that filters out the air, something that's purpose is so good, there's a noise that is so treacherous, it can drown even the strongest of hearts. That slow creak to a sudden crash of a clank occurs over and over. There's someone coming to get me.

He just cut the power and climbed back up into the attic. What if it's a girl? I'm even more afraid of a girl overpowering me and outsmarting me. It must be the male instinct that was brew in me for that little bit of time. Dear God, what can I do?

A knife! I need to get a knife from the kitchen. And a flashlight! I need to get a flashlight from my room. No one has come and killed me, yet.

I need to find a simple spot to defend myself from this tranquil darkness that has disturbed the usual rustic night. The bathroom, I'll go and hide in the bathroom. Well, not hide, but I'll lock myself in so that I can have an easier time to fight back.

Do I really want to fight back though? I mean, why? Why should I split minds with some man or woman that has decided to torture my life even more than it has been? Why should I care? Maybe I should, that this villain has come.

Nevertheless, here I am, in my bathroom, cowering at the thought of an over taker. I'd be the best person if someone ever tried to take over our country. Maybe I should join the Army.

No. I should not have to do this to myself. I don't need this crap. There's no one. No one there at all. Even if there is, let them take me. See if I care. I'm tired of this, and I'm tired in mind. Period.

I open the door and the lights flash on.

Damn. Damn, damn, damn. I hate this damn knife. I hate those damn lights. I hate this damn house with its damn attic. I hate this damned perfect weather. I hate this damned world.

I hate this loneliness.

I had to run. It was the only option. Everything I had in my life was gone. This was no dream. Everything was truly gone.

I ran.

I burst out of the house leaving the empty dial tone behind. I could hear it fade into the distance as I darted out of my yard. I didn't even shut the door.

As I ran barefoot through the dead grass, a sharp rock cut into my foot. I fell to the ground. Pulling myself up, I darted off again, only to take one step and run right into my brick mailbox.

I awoke with a pounding headache. The sun had only moved slightly down the horizon, so not much time had elapsed. I squinted to the fading dusk.

I still had to run. I was shaking. As I sprinted off down the road, my feet began to burn against the frozen asphalt. After about a hundred yards, I felt my feet no more.

The shaking wouldn't go away. It was not from the breathing or the tired muscles, it was something else. Something deeper inside me was burning, but it wouldn't come out.

I turned down another road; it was an old road. The asphalt was not as smooth, and my feet began to gain feeling again as the small pebbles in the road dug deeper into the soles.

The sun was almost completely gone. Soon darkness would overcome, and I would not know where to go. I kept running

The cold air began to take hold in my lungs. It burned down my throat and chilled my heart. The pain was soothing. It was all I had, and I stuck with it.

The sun was gone. I looked down on the road and looked behind me. Each step I took left a distinct shadow on the road. It was blood.

Each step cut deeper and deeper into my foot. I knew it would hurt like hell later, but that didn't matter. I needed the pain now. I needed more of it.

As I ran on down the road, my skin freezing down into my stomach, I tripped over something. I stumbled down the road a couple feet and finally came to a rolling stop. I couldn't feel anything on my body.

I crawled slowly back to what I had tripped over. There, in the middle of the road, in its own blood, was a cat. It looked dead; I thought it was dead. It took a breath.

I brought myself up over its body. I couldn't see what was wrong with it. It began to breathe hard, but with each breath came a cough. There was something coming out of its throat. It was blood.

"God, you've been hit. Oh God!" I muttered to the cat.

Damn drivers.

"I...I don't know what to do...look at me...look at me! Does it look like I can do anything?"

It coughed up more blood and let out a cry.

"Please...don't die...please...just hold on there."

It let out another cry and shifted its body to its other side. Something cracked.

"Oh God..."

I sat there huddled over the cat. A car drove up and slammed on its breaks, stopping a foot from my face.

"Hey, what are you doing in the road?" the driver said as he stepped out of his car.

He had an unconcerned attitude accompanied with a black business suit.

"I...it...a car must of..."

"Oh," he muttered as he saw the cat. "That your cat?"

"Uh...yeah...yeah it is," I lied.

"God man, I'm sorry. You want to take it to the vet or something?"

"My parents just died…I just got the call an hour ago…"

"Jesus man...Jesus…"

I read the *Bible* once. It took me about half a year, but I got through it. That was probably the last book that had a story so simplistic and so complex all at the same time, people just reached out to it. Scratch that. I guess there are all those other things like the *Koran* and *The Wizard of Oz*.

Books. What a waste of time. I've realize that in these past couple months, they keep coming up randomly throughout experience, like walking in my room, and there's one on the floor. Anyways, each time I step on one, it's just like ugh! I can't stand how it feels on my foot. And so I usually pick it up and throw it further off into the corner or under the bed.

So here I am now, standing with one foot uncomfortably atop of a small book, I'd say some two-hundred and fifty pages. Perhaps it will serve me an inspiring purpose. I always did find fire enjoyable.

Frankenstein by Mary Shelly. She, just like her husband, Percy Bysshe Shelly, was a total nut-case. Well, I guess there has to be some respect given to where respect has been earned to others. It just always seems to me that if you're going to come from a family with a history of one thing, you're not going to want to follow that psychological path. Like I don't want to die as my family did, so I don't understand why the Shelly family all decided to act as they did. Genetics sure are something.

Maybe they had some sort of gathering to plan out the future of their family. What if all the literature was really found in some vault that had been locked for years, and they decided to make some money off of it? Of course this is preposterous, just as the monster is, but at least the monster went down for Victor's own death. Seems right. A waste of time, yes reading is.

Literature is. I've found that now. It's all one big waste of time. Another plot that goes back long and long ago to just get us to sit still and keep our mouths shut. Besides, I don't see the joy in reading about some other man's horrors, when I have horrors of my own. And how much of the things they write in books actually come true? How much of it is even logical? None! It's all just a bunch of crap. That's what I think. That's what I know.

Later that night I would end up running from house to house trying to find the owner of the cat. The business man took the cat in his car. It was hard to get out of going with him. He kept insisting and insisting, but it wasn't my cat. I had to find the owner of the cat. I had to find whose life I had claimed as my property.

Finally after debating for fifteen minutes, I talked my way out of going with him. I told him I had to get home, and I lived right down the street. The doctors were waiting for me to call or something like that. The man drove off down the road into the glow of the moon, with my cat in his car.

I didn't know where to start. There I was, once again alone, and I had over twenty houses to go to. Surely one of these houses would know whose cat it was. Out of twenty houses, only nine had lights on.

I decided to go to the brightest house first. It had its porch lights on with some hut-like lights down the driveway. I approached the front door and peered through the tiny window. There was a dark shadow on the couch. I knocked.

A man came to the door. He had a chubby face, and he was holding a fried chicken leg. He looked at me as if to say, "what'chu want?" I looked back, waiting for a greeting. There came none. It was disgusting.

"Yes, I'm sorry for interrupting you at this time of night, but I was walking through the neighborhood, and..."

"Get to the point. What are you selling?" he sneered.

"Nothing, I was just walking through and this..."

"Look, I'm busy, so if you could just come back at another time or just not at all, that'd be great," he said as a piece of chicken rolled out of his mouth and down his shirt.

"God, just shut up and listen for a damn second!"

That got his attention.

"All I want to know is if you own a cat, but judging by the looks of things, if you did own a cat, it would probably be at the bottom of your stomach."

He swallowed. His Adam's apple moved up and down slowly along the indent of his throat.

"Look, there was a cat hit in the middle of the road and I was only trying to see if you knew whose it might be."

He looked at me dumbfounded.

"God..."

I walked on to the next house. There was a bright lighting coming from inside the house. It shined out the door. I walked up and knocked. An elderly woman came to the door with a slight smile.

"How might I help you, young man?" she said.

"Hi, I'm sorry to bother you so late..."

"It's fine," she leaned in and whispered, "My husband and I don't sleep much at night anyway."

"Alright, well, I was wondering if you owned a cat or knew anyone who owned a cat."

A dog barked in the background.

The elderly woman turned her head and yelled, "Hubby! I'll be there in a little bit!"

The dog barked back.

"No, I'm sorry I don't have a cat," she said.

"Do you know anyone who owns a cat?"

"No, I'm sorry, I don't," she smiled. "Any reason?"

"No, not really," I lied. "Thanks anyway."

"Uh-huh. Any time."

Two houses down and not a single idea of any cat. These were the homes I depended the most on. They were the ones with the brightest lights, the most hope. Nevertheless, I had to continue on, even if it meant looking in the darkest corners.

I went to every single house I could find nearby that night. Nothing. Absolutely nothing. It's like people had no relations to cats anymore. Made me feel kind of sorry for the generations of Pharaohs who worshiped those clever (and sometimes lazy) beasts. How could it come to something as desperate as this? The last hope for all of the cat-kind, and I was down to one house.

No lights. No lights at all around this house. It was a crummy little shack with moss and leaves al cluttered up in the gutters. One match and the thing would burn down in five seconds. Too bad I didn't have any matches...

I knocked. I knocked again. I knocked a third time. A spider moved across its silky blanket. It was a rather quite large spider, but I was larger. Nothing.

I stood outside that house for an hour. Part of the time was for me. I lost thought of the cat. Instead I sat down and watched as the spider crawled onto my leg. Through the pulsing moonlight, I saw a single strand of silk attach to my skin. It stood there, alone when the spider returned to its place. One single strand holding me down on the ground. If I moved, I was afraid the spider would fall and either land on me and bite me or fall to its own death (the one foot drop was quite deathly to the spider). So I sat there. Not thinking about the cat. Not thinking about my feet. Not thinking about...well, not thinking at all. What else was there to think about?

God I'm so bored. It's just one of those times, you know, when you're sitting all at home alone, and all that there's left to do is to move about aimlessly from one small task to another, but ultimately you accomplish nothing in your life, or in that day rather. What's the difference, eh? One day down the drain is just the same as a lifetime wasted away right? I've wasted many lifetimes; I've wasted many days.

Today I have raised myself out of bed, eaten breakfast, however nothing seemed to fill my filled stomach, so I laid back down on the couch, which coincidentally is where I currently stand, or sit rather. Fun times, eh? I just press and hold the seven.

Ring, ring, ring.

"Hello?" she asks.

"Kaitlyn, it's me. I need something to do."

"Okay, I'm kinda busy right now, but why don't you find some other people?" she says.

Sure, some other people. Let me just pull the shovel and pail out of my ass and build a giant sand-castle of friends.

"Who might I ask?" I ask.

"I don't know. What are you looking to do?"

"I don't know. What do you think I should do?"

"I don't know. What do you feel like right now?"

"I don't know. I'm bored."

"Have a party."

"Sure, a party. Who will come to this party?"

I sit up. There's that fish. We could have a party. Bubble, bubble, bubble.

"I'll call some people. How's say nine tonight?"

"Sounds great!"

There's a tone.

"Kaitlyn?"

Oh well. I still have three hours. Three hours until nine o'clock. Logically one would assume that means it's six. The only problem with that is the clock I use and that little thing of Einstein: Relativity. What a great thing it is. When ever you're having a great time, the time flies by extremely fast as to keep the fun time from ending early and leaving you with nothing but those awkward silences and times of boredom, kind of like now, except there's no fun involved. That's the boredom. This is where the other side comes in with relativity. Every time you are extremely tired of watching the clock hands tick and tock, relativity allows the time to pass slowly, which makes it much easier to count the ticks and tocks.

Tick tock, tick tock.

Ever so often the people mock,

Tock tick, tock tick.

The coughing blood of the sick.

Someone taught me that little ditty at some time in my life. Either that or I completely made it up. Who's to say? I always have this vision of going to some mountain and seeing this old raggedy man. He'd be a kind man, but he'd be extremely harsh in his wisdom. This would reflect in his physical structure as well. He'd have a soft voice but with striking diction. He'd have fine hair but of a coarse white. His skin would be soft but riddled with wrinkles. This would be the man I would go to see when I had a question about life. He'd be the coded truth.

And so I would ask him, "What does time have to do with any of this. I mean, there are people out there dying!"

This would follow some dramatic build up where all I had in life was the hope of saving the world. I would have just climbed for three days up this mountain, and I would come to the cave where this wise man sits and ask that question. This would lead to his cryptic response after, of course, a second to consider the situation.

"Tick tock, tick tock.

Ever so often the people mock,

Tock tick, tock tick.

The coughing blood of the sick."

And in that moment all would be right. Somehow in all the misunderstanding and questions I could have with this riddle, I would know the answer. I wish all things were that easy.

Tick tock, look at the time. It's already nine. That's what happens in relativity. I wonder who'll come. I wonder how many will show. Surely I'll have somewhere around ten. Kaitlyn knows I don't like too many people, but too little can also be awkward. I'll put my money on ten.

9:15. Hmm. There's no one yet. I walk around getting anxieties about the situations. I hope Kaitlyn's alright. I'll check my phone.

One missed call. It was Kaitlyn. Redial.

"Kaitlyn, hey, it's me. Where are you?"

"Oh, hey sorry, look, something came up and I can't be there, isn't there anyone there? I told them eight like we had decided."

"I thought we had said nine. Either way, there's no one here."

"Oh. Well I have to go, so I guess I'll see you later!"

"Ok…"

Silence.

"Bye?"

Silence.

Well, this has never happened. Hmm…I wonder what has gotten around this town that no one comes to a party. I guess someone passed some sort of warning around about me. But what would they warn about? I'm perfectly normal aren't I?

This has truly never happened before. Relatively speaking, I'll go to bed.

My parents threw this big bash for their anniversary. They had been married somewhere around fifteen years. It was one of those years that, for some odd reason, you throw a celebration for it. It's funny how birthdays are looked at with how much you can do with the coming of age, what is gained: driving at 16 (legally), voting and buying adult things at 18 (legally), drinking at 21 (legally). What accomplishments are there that define a marriage? Time. And so it is only with time that a marriage gains respect.

Fifteen years is a long time, more than half my life, which makes for good reason to throw a celebration of unity, love, and children. It was a nice party, a gathering of about thirty random people that my brother and I just nodded at when asked if we remember this or that. Yeah, sure, of course we remember that office. I mean, offices make such an impression of children.

So there my brother and I are at our home, thrown in the mix of adults. And of course in the mix of adults there is alcohol. It was one of those, to what we've done, cheers! Well my brother and I felt like we had done quite a lot too. They celebrated putting up with each other, and we celebrated putting up with them.

When the clock struck ten, a sudden sleepy feeling came over me like a foot being kicked in my ass, sending me to my room. My brother amazingly had the same feeling. Must be a brotherly bond, so we went with it. We surely weren't going to let the adults have all the fun. We would have more fun locked away in my room.

After about an hour of intense cooperation, our tent was complete. It was actually quite the accomplishment that required everything from searching for supplies in a rainy forest to visualizing what should be designed on a computer in your head. Man is better than the machine, or at least the man who built the machine.

"So what do we do now?" I asked my brother.

"Now, we wait for the giant beast to come, and then we will attack. Just listen, do you hear it?" he asked.

"I don't hear anything, except the rain of course, which is getting really heavy outside," I pointed out.

"Sh! You have to zone the rain sound out of your head and focus on your goal. I want to hear the sounds coming from there," he said pointing to the door.

I sat there for five minutes, listening intently to what was supposed to be the coming of a giant beast. There was nothing. Just when I was going to complain, I heard it. A snap and then a step. A tap and then a knock. A knock?

"You kids in there together?" my dad yelled through the door.

"Yeah, and we were sleeping until you said something!" my brother yelled back, acting as if being awoken.

"Oh, sorry. Well good. Go back to bed," my dad commanded.

Then the knock and tap and step and snap went away and I was back alone under all the sheets and chairs in the room with my brother.

"I don't understand how he expects us to sleep with that pounding music," my brother complained.

"I think it's peaceful," I said back, obviously lying.

"Yeah, it's peaceful. I'm getting tired. Mind if I just sleep here? I like it under the stars."

"Sure," I said to the forming stars of my imagination.

Well, it's a new day. The birds are chirping, the grass is glowing…oh what can I do on a day such as this? I go and get my phone, press and hold the number seven, and wait as it rings.

Ring. Ring. Ring.

"Hey, it's Kaitlyn. Leave a message if you have something to say. If not, don't."

Beep.

"Hey, it's me. I have something to say. First off, why the hell aren't you picking up your phone on a new day? I just woke up and I'm ready for a full day of fun. I don't think you have any reason to not call me back, or to not listen to this. What if it was important? Huh? What would you do --"

Beep.

"Your message has expired, thank you," says the little computer lady on the other end.

Ring. Ring. Ring.

"Hey, it's Kaitlyn. Leave a message if you have something to say. If not, don't."

Beep.

"Me again. Kaitlyn, I don't appreciate being cut off. You'll have to get onto your phone company about that. What was I saying? Hmm...oh yeah! You need to pick up. It's no emergency, I don't know if I said there was an emergency. There's not. Just me. Alone. At home. It's Saturday. You know what I'm thinking. I have everything. Just bring a stomach and we'll make it a night, eh?"

Beep.

"Your message has expired, thank you," says the little computer lady on the other end.

Damn you computer lady. How rude you are, but how nice you sound. How could I ever be mad at you?

Well, Kaitlyn isn't answering. What do I do?

I go to the pantry and pull out a bottle of rum. Just a little will be good to get the blood flowing. It's is a bit chilly. I pour some into a cup and put the bottle away.

I walk to the door. Sure it's early in the day, but I believe in starting things as quick as I can. Procrastinations not my style.

I open the door. It's pitch black outside. Whoa! What time is it? The clock says two. Wow. It's two in the morning. I take a sip. It's great to be outside. The bats are screeching, the bugs are biting...this is what I do on a night such as this.

Well, back inside where I'm not going to die from a lack of blood.

I turn the lights off. How could I have missed that it was dark outside. Oh well. The only light that glows is the faint whisper of life from the fish aquariums. They tricked me. I'll blame it on the fish.

Speaking of the fish tanks, they look disgustingly filthy, and I can tell that from across the room. Something's not right. When was the last time I cleaned them? I can't even remember.

I set my drink down on the counter and walk over to the tanks.

"Fishies want to be cleaned?" I say like speaking to a baby, "Yes you do. Daddy thinks you do. So are you going to cooperate with me? Good fishies."

I'll start with the top first.

Grabbing all the necessary supplies from about the house, I actually get some energy flowing. What am I working with here? This tank is definitely going to need the full cleaning. This means taking the fish out, taking the water out, taking the plants out, taking the life out.

Thank God we aren't removed from the city when they clean that at night, if they really do what they say.

I remove the top fixture to the tank and begin to siphon out the water. There's a short hose that I have to suck on one end to get the water going. For the cost of drinking a little fish water, there's no need for the good old fashioned bucket. I forgot how yummy that water tastes.

After the water is down about halfway, I shift the hose over to a bucket, so I have somewhere to put the fish. Then I take the plastic plants out and grab the fish net.

"Ok, little fishies, just stay calm."

They don't listen to me. After wrestling around for a good thirty minutes, I get all the fish out. Then I drain the rest of the water; there's no point in carry more weight then I need to.

Now, should I do this one first or work so the bottom tank is done at the same time? That tank is absolutely disgusting. I can barely see into it, there's so much slime and algae growing on the glass. I'm not even sure if there's anything alive in there.

I look around inside the tank for a little bit and then see it. Sitting in the dark corner is that one fish. It's gotten to be quite large, but still as black as night. And its eyes are still that same cloudy blue. How murky and evil they look just staring at me. It doesn't move. I take a step back. It moves closer towards me. I take another step back, right into the bucket holding all the other fish.

It knocks over and all the fish spill out. As the water spreads through the carpet, the fish are left to flap helplessly.

I take a quick glance and the beast in the bottom tank. Its mouth is cracked open as if to hold an evil grin. I try to grab the fish on the floor, but I slip and fall on my back. Smoosh.

How could it be that all of them were under my back? All three of them just killed like that. Just like that, dead. I get up, but can't look down at their bodies. I glare at the beast.

"You did this, you know that. It was your fault! And now they're dead, and you're all alone. Forget it if you expect me to help you now."

I pick the three bodies up and go plop them in the toilet and flush. The massacre has ended. You all die with honors. I grab some towels and go soak up the water. I could use a shower, so I head to the bathroom. There's a splash off in the distance.

I remember this one time, sometime in my memory sitting after the car crash and the cat incident, I took a bath. Simple process, yes, I know, but this was different. It was nice and relaxing. I usually take showers, but when I feel the need of de-stressing, I take a bath and add some bubbles (they're fun to play with).

I had this book. Some book someone had bought me. A self-help-how-to-get-through-deaths kind of book. I promised I would read it, so I did for about five minutes.

I sat down in the tub and read as the water climbed to the edge. Within the last minute, before the water would overflow, I turned the heat up all the way, so the water would stay warm for a little bit after being off. Of course, this whole process was completed with my feet, as I myself had been reading.

Flipping the faucet off with a quick jab of my right foot, I continued reading. Somewhere between "how to tell others" and "how you should react to their reaction of your reaction to the death" I saw through the slip of an eyelet the pages of the book sink slowly into the water...

...when I woke up, surprisingly the book hadn't molded and spread though out the tub like fish food. Instead, it had just kind of expanded its normal size by an inch. So much for that promise. I threw the book aside and sat up in the tub.

"I wonder how much time has passed," I thought to myself.

Slowly shifting up in the tub so my back was against the wall, I felt a strange sensation in my hands and legs. It was almost a soft feeling, but then I took my hands out of the water.

They looked different -- very much different. No longer had I the hands of a younger man, now I had the hands of a marshmallow. Each time I bent my fingers, a sharp sense of tightness shot to my brain, and I winced inside. I decided the water wasn't the best place to sit in, considering, so I began to get up.

I struggled. My legs were weak. When I finally managed to pull myself up a little, my right knee buckled under. God damn that hurt!

I stepped out of the tub and felt a rush of blood to several parts of my body, even though it felt as if these places had enough weight to them. Hmm...my face looked different. It was darker and had a slight wrinkle that seemed to infect every crease on my face. My hands were like potato sacks. I needed a cane to walk it hurt so badly. I had changed. I had changed and I didn't want to. I had no control over it. I had gone to sleep at one time, only to wake up at another a changed man, an older man. These were not wrinkles I wanted to bear, but it seemed I had no choice.

Split second decisions often mean the difference between life and death. No one ever thinks about how venerable we are as children, just because the ability to make those split second decisions is so jerky. Think about how easy it is to walk and skip and jump. Then watch a five-year-old walk, skip, and jump. The simple lack of coordination is comical, but ceasing when the realization sinks on of aging: returning to that simplistic childish coordination, only this time there is a lack of energy.

That's why you have to live life fast and hard while you have the youth, so you can make those split second decisions without reserve of shaking as you cut up a carrot.

I think I'll go to a wedding. It's been a while since I've been to one. Actually, the only memory of a wedding that I hold is of my own parents, but that's only through the photos and short stories told by tongue. I've never been to a wedding.

There. Split second decision to save my life. Going to some random wedding will save me the embarrassment of not knowing what is going on at one that I'm required to go to, like my own, which will indeed never happen, for I will never get married. They say never to say never. I say I will never get married. Why would I? I'm not that type of person. Sure I could give unconditional love and all that fifty-fifty crap, but I don't think I could raise a family. I don't think I could wish my burden onto the back of another person.

The newspaper tells of a wedding on Saturday at this old church in town. It starts at 3 PM. Let's see, what's today? Saturday. That figures. What time is it? 12 PM. Wonderful. What are the odds someone will be getting married at the same time I desire to witness the classic ritual of matrimony? Probably two in one. People these days just seem to pop the question , pop some champagne, and then pop out a baby. Or two.

Let's see, I've got my tux. Simple black and white from the funeral. It was a dressy occasion, a celebration they say. And let me tell you, it was quite the party. It was about as fun as being the only sober person a party, just when your life is feeling really shitty, but still you end up being the only one without any fun, because that's what the fun of those parties come from. It's a lot like weddings.

No one goes to a wedding to see a ceremony. No one gets married so that they can look into the eyes of another person and just gaze on and on as if to lose themselves in an illusion of infatuation that ultimately ends up to be more directed toward the self. That's why I think it's hard to find someone to marry these days. Everyone expects the normal, when the normal just keeps rising. It's impossible to find someone to marry at thirteen, buy some old farm in the country, and raise a twelve child family with crops and animals. That's a real family.

The country's a great place to have a wedding too, or at least the reception. But still people have to stick with the traditions of their parent's parents, so the wedding takes place at a church.

At least this is a nice church. I hate those churches that don't have stained glass windows. It really doesn't matter what the picture on the windows are, it's more of the colors. I think even a blind man can sense the tranquility of the rain bowed lights. I like to squint my eyes to blur the images as the light shines through. The sun slowly fades in and out, but the entire time a striking blur of illusion plays with my mind. It's like drugs in church.

Ah, here comes the bride, there goes the bride, everyone's a bride, look how the groom does hide! It's pitiful. Honestly, I think the thing that gets under me the most is the candles in the back. Right at the bottom of the flame, there's a murky blue haze. It's trapping me in. It's like eyes. Two candles right next to each other: unity. Two eyes glaring down upon me, tempting me, scowling me, mocking me, hating me, fearing me, taking me in so that the entire world around just disappears. The blasted beast has struck again. My heart is speeding up and I'm sweating profusely.

"Are you okay?" a little old lady whispers to me as she sees water dripping down my face.

"What? Yeah. Huh? Oh..." I say taking the handkerchief out of my pocket and wiping my face, "Sometimes these things just build up so much happiness and sorrow all at the same time."

She nods in agreement and looks at her husband. I wonder if she has any regrets...

I wonder if I can sneak my way into the reception. Normally those things are planned out and there's no room for someone to just come on their own accord. Well, I am the cousin of the uncle of little Susie's best friend's mother who went to college with Bethany...or something like that.

What do you know? I follow a couple cars, turns out the reception is at some old time farm house that's been renovated. Actually remodeled as of April 28, as the sign proudly states outside.

I love these things. If only the youth of every town would realize the alcohol was so easily accessible at these functions. Happy times mean happy people, which means free drinks all around. I guess if more people did realize this vital manipulation, I would be put out of business. Maybe I should start a business out of this, while no one else is in the field.

I think the music they play at weddings is the best. Weddings have everything from the classics to just a little spritzer of modern times to keep the youth happy. Honestly, past a certain point the DJ could put on songs about the jungle and everyone would dance to it as if it were an '80s' groove.

One song after another, I'm losing myself to the crowd. It's such a vibrant clash of worry-free lovers; most of the ladies are looking for someone to hold tight, as an extreme case of jealousy sinks over half the bridesmaids at the sight of their friend happy with a man. Is it wrong to take advantage of this. I don't think it's technically taking advantage if you're only dancing.

Dancing leads to more drinking. More drinking leads to more dancing. And somewhere in the midst of things I swear I feel lips brush my own. No, I can't do that, but everything is blurring left and right. I wonder how I'll get home.

It's all done. I'm walking with some girl in a pretty dress. Don't know her name. Don't really know my own name. I don't think we care. Am I driving? I can't drive. She's not driving. Looks like it's my car. I think we go for about 100 yards before pulling off into some driveway into the woods. It's better not to drive in this state anyways.

I've only slept out in the car one time in my entire life. My family was out camping, tent and all, which is the only real way to camp. I believe we were up somewhere in West Virginia. It was spring time, but the sky had been cloudy the entire day.

After a full day of activities (we would always leave early in the morning to get there by lunch, so then we would have the entire afternoon to goof around on wild trails and see who could keep their feet in freezing cold stream-water the longest. I won that one…but I got sick about a week later), it was just a typical vacation-camping day for us.

And so when the area was scouted out, we returned to the camp to get some wood to build a fire, always done with flint; my brother loved to show off his magical rocks and start a fire. I was impressed. Too bad I later found out what it was. Sometimes the truth ruins the wonder of childhood. The truth always ruins the wonder of childhood. But I suppose it's better to live by the truth than to live in a world of lies, depends on how much you can make yourself believe.

And so night time fell, as it always does when the day is over. I believe we had just finished setting up the tent with all the poles in some formation that made sense to the older mind. My brother was working the fire onto the wood. He had brought some lent along, and he quickly brought that ablaze. Blowing on it to keep it up, he moved it to under the little teepee of wood he had constructed. The fire slowly climbed up through some leaves and smaller branches and made it's way to the larger branches. Drip.

Something hit my face. Drip. Another one. Before the fire even had a chance to get steady, a thunderstorm erupted in splashes all around. I believe it must have been comical to the elderly couple with their RV, as they watched our pitiful family struggle to make it into the tent, only to realize the water was just gushing in a giant hole in the top. A tree branch had fallen straight through.

And so we dashed off to the car, leaving everything except the blankets we grabbed back in the tent. As we got inside, we quickly wrapped up in the damp blankets to warm ourselves up (now that I remember, I wasn't the only one to get sick later). My dad was in the drivers seat, my mom in the passenger seat, and my brother and I in the backseat. One big happy family all in the car together.

As the lightning and thunder poured out around us, we felt safe in the vehicle. We were all there together. I remember swapping different scary stories. My brother always had the best, well the best in the eyes of a child.

"It was a dark and stormy night in Claudeville. A normal night in the town of strange happenings. Two little children found themselves outside as the dark clouds rumbled over. Suddenly, a man appeared and asked for help. He needed a child to come with him. The two kids decided it was alright and followed the man. When they got to a bridge, the man said he only needed one child, so he grabbed one and threw the other into the river. Suddenly the man started shining a great green, as did the river, and the souls of those came pouring out over the bank. The man pushed the child down into the earth as the glop from his decaying body went drip, drip, drip. And as the child's face was pushed down, down, down, he slowly felt a tingle coming up, up, up from the earth. It was the light coming for him. He tried to resist, but gave in as the light came closer, and closer, and closer, and…BOO!"

I don't think I got much sleep that night. I'm not sure any of us did. It wasn't the best place to try and sleep. It took some time, but eventually we fell asleep.

Ah. A subtle little yawn. I squirm a little. Something's in the car with me. Oh, it's a girl. But where am I? I feel so refreshed. What time is it. 6:00 AM. Wow, we must've gone to sleep early. I feel like I've slept forever. Best damn night of sleep I've ever had.

"Hey, you awake?" I ask the girl whose dress is crinkled all over.

Her face is in the seat.

"Huh…oh, yeah."

"You want me to take you to your car?" I ask, trying to be polite.

"Huh…oh, yeah. Sure."

And so we drive the 100 yards back to her car. She stares off and out the window, as I try and focus on the task of driving I'm really not interested in. It's a nice thirty second drive with each other.

I pull up next to the only car in the parking area. She starts to get out.

"Can I at least get your name or something?" I ask.

"I don't…I don't think it really matters…"

And with that she shuts the door and gets into her car and drives off. I shrug my shoulders. She's right. It doesn't really matter. So I drive home. There's a friend I've been meaning to see.

Ring. Ring. Ring.

"Kaitlyn…oh Kaitlyn, where for art thou Kaitlyn?" I ask.

"Right Cheer!"

"Well it's about damn time you picked up! I've been calling you all morning. Please tell me you haven't been asleep this entire time…anyway it's not important because now we're talking and you finally picked up. How are you?"

"I'm tired" she replies, "and this is the first time you've called."

"That's nice. You know how much sleep I got last night? I'll tell you. Well, I'm not really sure, but it feels like days. God, I'm ready to go climb a mountain."

"That's too cliché for the morning. If you expect me to be awake, you need to at least do something interesting. I was up late last night…"

"Oh yeah. What were you doing?" I ask.

"Nothing…just out," she says.

"Out?"

"Out."

"Out, like out?

"Out, yes."

"Like out with --"

"I was out damnit! What do you want?" she says annoyed.

"Jeez, what's gotten into you? You've seemed so distant these past couple of days."

"Look, I'm sorry, I've just been, around. Do you want to give me a chance to make it up?"

"Well only if you tell me what happened," I demand.

"Okay. I'll tell you."

Dial-tone.

Wonderful. Well I wonder when she'll decide to grace me with her presence. Hopefully before the moon crashes into the earth (which will occur in 935,124,098,127,401,158,132,598,172,948,172,498,129,482 days, 6 hours, and 37 minutes).

There's a knock in the fish aquarium. Damn fish. I walk to the aquarium and look straight down. The water level is bobbling back and forth. Hmm…that fish is a little feisty today. Must be the change in the weather.

There's a knock at the door. I walk to it and open it up.

"Wow. That was quick."

"Glad to see you too," Kaitlyn says as she steps in, deciding finally to grace me with her presence.

That's okay. I'll forgive her. She's too beautiful not to forgive.

"Alright. Well give me the scoop of what's going on. Why have you been so distant?" I ask.

"Look. I really don't know how to explain this. It's truly going to be difficult for us both to understand. You know I'll always be here for you whenever you need me for whatever you need me."

"Wonderful, same here to you," I say.

She pulls a bottle out of her purse.

"Can we get a little to drink first?" she asks. Hinting at the need.

I get the cups. She pours out some drinks. Pineapple rum, a little something tropical. Not to bad, and ah! Goes down smoothly.

"Okay, here's the deal," Kaitlyn begins as if about to go into a long speech, "This is going to be difficult to say. So here, I'm just going to come out and say it. Ever since you dropped out of school, we've done a pretty good job at staying close together. And I'm not saying I'm breaking things off as your friend, because I'm not. I'm just saying that I know, looking into the future, things are going to get extremely difficult with the ending semesters coming up. And this is a big deal for my family and I, I mean you know how much my parents...how much they wanted me to go though this and gain the opportunities that you'll...that you'll never have. All I'm trying to say is that, if you truly want to keep hanging out all the time, I need you to help me out some more. There are people who don't know you and know me, and I hang out with them without you, and I want you to get out more and come to our parties, because they are fun. I just feel like you're so detached, you know. I just think you need to get yourself out there more. I'm not going to help you do that, because honestly I don't know if I can do that."

A tear forms in her eye.

"And it really scares me that I can't help you like that, because I know what you've been through, and I've tried to be here for you every single day of your life, but there are other people out there. There's a whole nother world out there that you're just throwing away. And I hate to see you do that, because you're such a great kid. And even though you've gone through so much shit, you've developed into a fairly decent young man."

I'm shocked.

"Thanks mom" I say.

"Don't say that. I'm not your mother. I'm just another friend. No one will ever replace your mother."

"I know."

"Do you? Do you know that? I mean, sometimes I don't understand it! You don't even act like they're dead. Your parents are dead! And you're just sitting here alone all the time. Do something! They're dead. They're gone..."

With this, she moves slowly to the door, backing away as the tears begin to fall. She leaves. The door clicks softly behind her shadow. I get the feeling she feels it a little more that I do. What was she talking about? Why was she crying? What was she crying for?

And there's the lone bottle of rum still sitting right on the counter where Kailtlyn left it. Ah...what the hell...

One of the only times I can remember being allowed to legally drink alcohol in my own house was at New Years. When I say legally, I mean by the governing laws of mom and dad. It's really that simple relationship that establishes all the laws in this world. Think about it. As soon as you're born, you have someone looking over you. As you grow up, that someone spreads to the general adult population. And as time goes then, it shifts to those above you, ultimately landing in the true legal system. It's kind of true that laws from parents are laws. It's like the transitive property. That's from geometry.

New Years for the millennium was quite the celebration. There was such a sense of accomplishment for the human race. For two thousand years we had developed some relative system to which we measured our own passing. And behind all this power of good, there was the power of evil. Everyone had a lingering fear of the computers. It was comical to hear people joke about it, because deep down they were just covering up their own ignorance. That's understandable.

It was quite the gathering. Everyone had come to our house to send 1999 off and say hello to the triple 0 with a two in front. For me, it was just another party with alcohol. I guess the only thing that makes it different is the damn confetti. No matter what tactic is used, it always ends up in your cup and ultimately in your stomach. Not that many people keep their stomachs down that night anyway.

Well, this one was different for another reason as well. As my parents were pouring the drinks, they had a little some themselves as well.

"Sons," my dad said, coming at us with two cups, "The rules are still the same around here."

He set the two cups down and walked away, back into the crowd of adults. Living in the Eastern Time zone gives quite the advantage when it comes to being the first in the states to celebrate. Everyone is watching your parties on TV (not that ours was filmed). It always does feel uplifting to be the first. Of course it wasn't a desire, it was merely a coincidence. If we wanted to celebrate first, we would've gone on some cruise ship. I think they were also the last to celebrate as well. I've always thought time zones were crazy anyway.

So logically thinking about it, my brother and I each took a cup and sniffed it.

"What is it?" I asked him.

"Smells like Champagne. Don't worry, it's not that strong," he said.

We had five minutes before the count down, so we went ahead and downed them right there. My dad must have seen this, because he came over to talk to us. Thinking we were about to die, my brother and I put our heads down.

"Why don't you save these for the actual countdown, okay?" he said handing us two new cups.

"Okay!" we responded together.

It was amazing. How on earth could this be happening to us? I mean, our parents were never like that.

"Do you think he's really had that much to drink?" I asked my brother.

"I guess so!"

And so we sat there in total amazement until the countdown. 10….9…8…7…6…5…4…3…2…1…and the lights went out.

A couple people screamed, but most of the people were to caught up in the cheer of Happy New Year! I only chugged down my cup of Champagne. When the lights came back on, it was really only some older man trying to scare everyone. We all had a good laugh.

I set down my empty cup on the table. Apparently my brother had done the same thing that I had, because his cup was also empty. I felt different. I didn't know what it was, but suddenly everything got really light. My brother must have been feeling it too, because he just smiled at me. Then we both started to laugh at nothing.

The rest of the night we went around tipsy and high with our newfound experience. We made complete fools out of ourselves, but everyone still laughed when the lamp was knocked over, and when my brother tripped and fell on the floor.

It was about an hour later when my mom came up to us and said it was time for bed. With little protest, we followed and headed off to our rooms. I fell asleep faster than I expected, but it was much needed.

Then next morning, I woke up as happy and cheerful as ever. My brother felt the same. Mom and dad on the other hand looked absolutely horrified. Their eyes were squinted and their heads shaky. I don't think the state of the house made it any easier.

"What's wrong mom?" my brother joked.

"I guess they can't handle their drinks," I whispered to my brother.

My dad walked up to us, looked at us, and laughed. He then walked over to the refrigerator and pulled out a bottle. He poured some into a cup and started drinking it.

"You know," he said after finished swallowing, "sparkling grape juice taste really good in the morning. You should try it dear."

Mickey Bahr

I find myself having this reoccurring vision. I doubt I'm the only one to see this in their dreams or thoughts, because it's quite a common sight to anyone who drives a long distance in the south. In the south, you can't go more than 24 hours without having some sort of precipitation. Whether it's rain from the sky, water from a hose, or spit from someone chewing dip, the skies are always shaping and morphing. It's a rather beautiful site.

My vision would be beautiful for anyone that doesn't have it over and over, or know the significance of it. The sights really aren't that great for me though. Driving. I'm always driving. And of course, it's raining outside, normal rain for a while, a nice nighttime shower.

Signs flutter off in the distant slowly passing as blurs to my right. I'm actually interested in what they say, but my curse is the inability of focus. And so the blurs stream by side to back, side to back, side to back, side to back.

As I continue down the road, the rain slowly picks up and my windshield wipers respectively slow down. Sometimes I can feel the water in my eyes like being pulled through a river. The pain of moisture in my eyes is fluctuating from sight to black, a complete darkness.

I take my hands off the wheel, and the car continues down its own path, like I never was driving it before. Just as I can see a blur of green from a sign telling my destination, the vehicle takes a sharp cut across the road dodges some cars, and then slams into the ditch.

Total darkness.

It's a black so strange, so unreal. No one is ever in complete darkness. Even when you go into the Marianna Caverns and they shut out the lights, there's still some glow of radiance that allows another sense to kick in and feel the others.

Total darkness holds no light.

Even when your eyes are shut, there's an image imprinted in your mind of the last situation of the room. There's still a constant glow from the surviving colors.

Total darkness holds no rainbows.

Even when you die, there are still the lights of the future forever embedded in your heart.

Total darkness holds no hope.

I've only experienced it once in a worldly situation that was not just some figment of my imagination. It was some time ago as a child. I was with my family, and we were playing around in a park. As my dad through a ball my way, I turned and saw something off in the distant.

For a single split second, I could see what it was. It was the most beautiful speck of a light you could imagine. As every color of the spectrum passed over my eye, I saw a flash of myself and then nothing.

Total darkness.

It took me about three days to heal from the ensuing concussion, the headaches and rather large bump. It took me about a year to get over the fear of that darkness.

And here I sit now, with the gloom of this darkness coming over again.

One day, such a long time ago, my brother and I were playing around on the school playground. It was just a regular summer afternoon. The sun was hot, the air was humid. We were wearing those classy Nike shorts and t-shirts, and we were sweating like pigs.

It was a great playground. Way back when it was legal to make playgrounds that gave splinters. This wood castle could keep us busy for hours upon hours. Our parents sat under the shade and chatted about life, while we ran around and killed each other.

If we were lucky, other kids might come along, but it just so happened that on this day we were alone. It was just us. Just us two. Our parents like this better, for there's less of a risk of some fight breaking out or some other childish nonsense. It's not like brothers fight at all.

The day started out nice and simple, just as any good day should. We went to the playground at lunch and had a little picnic. Peanut butter and jelly sandwiches were a gift from God back then (Now I stick with just the peanut butter. It's a nice healthy snack, full of protein). And to top this four-course meal off, Kool-Aid from a little water pitcher. It's nice to be prepared.

After the simple lunch, my brother and I picked up a game of pretend on the playground, while mom and dad sat back in the shade. Man it's a full time job being a parent.

I was the first mate, and of course my brother was the pirate-captain. We pretended that the sand was a giant sea of lava, and we were on a lava-proof boat.

"Ahoy there!" my brother called to me.

"Ay Captain!" I called back.

"It seems like there isn't much we can do. We're surrounded by our enemy. Have any ideas?" he asked.

"Sure. You can run over to that island and call for backup!" I said referring to the grass where the lava ended.

"That sounds like a great idea. But you should be the one to do it. Think how brave you would be, running across a sea of lava! Your people could never thank you enough," he said trying to inspire me into some heroic act.

"Ay! And captain, if I don't make it, send my love to my wife and kids at home."

"Good luck sailor!" he yelled to me.

And off I'd go running as fast as I could. It looked like I might make it. Almost there, almost, almost...Bam! Lights out.

I had hit my head straight into the parallel bars. I guess sometimes the lava is just too powerful.

Dear God my head hurts, and there's nothing I can do to stop it! It's this throbbing pain that keeps pushing and pushing and pushing until it feels as if my temples themselves are going to explode. Well, to be completely honest, there is something I can do, just not right at this second. At this second my head hurts, and the pain will not go away.

I'll take a shower. That might help. It never really helps me do anything, but maybe it will this time. I take two showers a day, but I could live without them all. After a while I would grow accustomed to the smell, so what's the point? I mean, yes it is quite a disgusting thought, but every time I take a shower, I just end up sweating or getting dirty or just not feeling clean, and there's nothing I can do about this. I'll still take my shower.

It's not so much of an operation or adventure for me as it is just a process. I have it timed down perfectly. They take a very long time to accomplish, but it's the same every time. I always end up clean in the same way, but only to get dirty.

I slip out of my boxers and toss them behind the door to retrieve after my shower. This is a trait learned as my mother did not want me to keep clothes out in the hall, just in case some guest arrived when I was in the shower (not like they'd be able to get in now). Nevertheless, my boxers come off and are thrown behind the door.

I turn the water on, but only to where it is running out of the faucet and not the shower head. I keep it cold, so I don't waste the hot water I'll use later. I like the sound of water. It's relaxing. I sit down on the green carpet rug and lay backwards. I just sit there and absorb the world around me. For a second, I feel the throb go away, but alas it returns. The following proceedings are a set of stretches I admit to differing each time, but this time my head hurts, so I stretch my neck, hoping it will magically help its weight from above. It doesn't, so I'm done with my stretching. I usually do some pushups or sit-ups or both, but I can't today. I know when I have a headache and try to do pushups; it's like banging a hammer to ring the bell at the fair. Each time I push down and up, my head rings back and forth with a high-pitched pressure that only I can hear. So I skip this step.

I step into the shower and close the curtain behind me. Reaching down with my right hand, I turn the handle to make the water warm -- it's just a simple twist to the left. Once my feet have felt the correct temperature, I pull the pin to start the shower and race to the back of the tub, as I know the first drops will be freezing. As I sit there in anticipation, the sound slowly transfers from the faucet to the shower-head. And then the water hits. It's never really as bad as I expect it to be, but perhaps one day I'll forget to expect it and find how cold the water truly is. I doubt this will ever happen; I don't forget.

I wash my hair first. I use some tea-tree shampoo, and then whatever brand of shampoo is up on the shelf above; my eyes are closed the whole time. I do this quickly, as I like the conditioner the best. It's the tube on the left and shampoo is on the right. That's the way it is. I squirt some conditioner onto my hand and rub it around to smother my tools. With nothing better to do, I just dive in. I like the silky feel of shampoo. It seems to soak into my head and drown out the throb. The feeling is priceless. I leave the conditioner in my hair to soak while I wash the rest of my body.

I use a bar of soap. I tried to use a liquid soap once, but the water washes it right off your hands. I never really found the point behind that. I begin with my neck and work down. It's very systematic but relaxing at the same time. I rejuvenate my neck, arms, chest, back, and all the way down to my toes on my feet. Throughout this process I am constantly washing my hands. Even though it is soap, I still feel it can get dirty from my own body. I still use the dirty soap to wash my hands though. As long as I don't think about it too much, I'm fine.

I set the bar of soap in the dish on the shelf opposing the shelf of the shampoos and conditioner. Now it's time for my face. I have two different types of face wash, but I have no idea what the difference is and what each one does for me; I still use them both. Holding both bottles in one hand, I proceed to squirt a little dab of each into my open hand. I don't like washing my face, but I guess it's a good thing to do. My mom always made sure I did.

After spreading across my face and "working it into my pores," as my mom liked to say, I just stand under the water and let it flow over my face. I then tilt my head down, so the conditioner washes out. And then back to the face. And to the head. To the face. Head. Face…until I'm dizzy as hell and ready to move on to the rest of my body. I use my hand this time to wipe off the water as it hits the various places on my body. After this boring part is finished, I dizzy myself out again with another head-to-face rinse off and proceed to turn of the water.

We can learn a lot from watching animals. One way to keep less water on the bathroom floor and in your towel is to shake like a dog. I do this each time, even with a headache. And while shaking violently and again getting quite dizzy, I wipe the water off my body as it falls from my hair. A gallon of water always goes down the drain.

And my shower is complete. It's too much work, which is why I guess ultimately I don't like them. Even after shaking, I still use the towel, just to get the dampness off my skin, so my clothes won't stick to me. I grab the towel from its hanger over the toilet and dry my hair. I wonder what it looks like now. I can't see anything, because the mirror is fogged up. I take the small towel by the sink and wipe a couple times across the mirror. My hair is a mess.

I move down my head to my neck, arms, chest, back…I turn to see my back in the mirror. The scars of self-flagellation still linger, etched into my skin.

The original purpose of whipping my own back was not as demented as the process infers. It was clear logic. I always had trouble working through pain, physical pain. I was usually pretty creative in finding a way to get around the ache in my head, but the pain of my body seemed to always exist, but I found ways to take it.

I had to take it. Ever since I was a young child, and my body ached, my parents would just look at each other and state "growing pains" for every time I uttered a solitary complaint. So I found ways to get by.

After a while, some types of pains just went away. I learned to block them out. It was a game I would play with myself sometimes. Who can ignore the gash in your leg the longest? In competing with myself, I guess I could neither win nor lose, and this goes in many directions as well.

I read about the history of self-flagellation on the computer once. I had just seen some flick about some religious men who did some stuff (other than whip themselves in the back). What can I say, I was intrigued? In this one article, it went beyond the religious high that many assume in this process of rips and tears of the skin; it went into science. I always thought there was a reason the world worked the way it did, so there was always a science of some kind there.

Apparently our body has these natural pain killers (would've been nice if mine functioned a little better), and these come out in many ways. Endorphins are released in severe injuries; it's what allows all those great movie scenes of the wounded soldier fighting on. It often abolishes all pain. Self-flagellation in historic times was a kind of modern steroid; it was a pain killer.

And so through this logic, I began the long process of whipping. I'm not quite sure why, but it was always forty lashes. I used this rubber cord and attached some paper clips and other various objects to the end. It swung hard and cut deep. It was perfect for working out.

But somewhere in that process I lost myself. I lost my logic. I changed myself unintentionally, and it was as if I had no control. It scared me. It honestly did. Each night I would kneel once after another to the hand of twinge; it was my own hand.

My dad always would let me put the star on the Christmas tree. He'd let my brother lend a hand, but my brother knew it was something special for me. I guess there's no choice of who does it now.

No more great trees from the patch, only one single four foot plastic tree from the remnants of mom and dad starting out in life. It's more logical to buy a tree to use over and over than pay for one that dies year after year.

Sure I can afford it, but what need do I have? I'm the only one looking at it. I have one tree, no lights, and a star on top. It's a nice star. Hopefully Kaitlyn will stop by and see the star. Maybe she'll look at me.

Christmas morning goes by and so does the afternoon. It's a normal day, excepting the slight dull of cheers from little kids across the way as they have their Christmas dreams come true. I don't really have those types of dreams anymore. What's the point? Who's going to play Santa? I guess I could do it myself, but playing chess with myself was never much of an appeal.

And so instead I set the table for two. One for me, and one for the ghosts of Christmas past, present, and future; all together wound up as my family in the mental sense, but as Kaitlyn in the physical sense, if she decides to come. I called her earlier, but I only could leave a message.

And so I sit at my kitchen table with some candles burning brightly, the flame flickering slowly left and right as the air currents shift about my head. They burn a bright yellow down to a cloudy blue. Kind of like the blue of those eyes. The candles are so close to each other. Two blue spots, two eyes. It's still there, moving at me, leaping across the table to get me.

I move my chair back into the corner, but I can't stop it. It's still coming. There's a ring at the door, but I can't move. It'll get me. I can't let the eyes get me. I can't let that damn fish get to me. The star is shining too bright on a night like this.

Too long of a time has passed for a simple fire to burn the memories of children born in the past. Great people they were. Great people we are. No matter how great of a world it may be, I cannot help it. The fire only creeps closer to burn down the plastic tree.

"What are you doing?"

Kaitlyn storms in to save me, at least, that is what it looks like to me. But maybe not, I never know these days. Perhaps she just wants to add to the fire.

"Hey, how's it going?" I ask.

"You're unbelievable!" she replies.

The next couple of seconds are a mix of me sitting in the corner as Kaitlyn runs into the garage to grab something, and somewhere in there a giant puff of white powder comes about.

"It's snowing on Christmas," I state nonchalantly.

"Look at me," Kaitlyn demands after the roundabout charade, "are you even sane anymore? Why are you doing this? Do you want to die?"

"What are you talking about?" I ask unconcerned.

I look around and see the surroundings of burnt wood, tree, and floor and the mush of extinguisher powder all about the room.

"Oh dear Lord…was that me?" I ask finally realizing what had happened.

"Are you drunk or something? I come in and you're just sitting in the corner mumbling to yourself, while the candles were tipped over burning up the entire room, or part of it. It doesn't matter, because through the whole thing you were just sitting there and if I hadn't come in on my own, I mean I rang and all, but you didn't come, and I saw the light and I couldn't just stand there and watch the --"

I lean over and kiss her.

"Merry Christmas," I state sincerely.

She looks confused.

"Oh, there's this mistletoe above us. I just…"

She understands now.

"You are one crazy kid," she states.

"Yeah, I guess I am. But hey! You're still here aren't you?"

"Yeah, I guess I am. I got your message, so here I am. Merry Christmas. What's for dinner?" she asks.

"Dinner? Oh…"

Suddenly we both smell the smoke coming from the kitchen.

"I think there's some ham in the oven."

"Wow. You just like to burn everything don't you? Okay. Well, I'll clean up here if you go deal with whatever is in the kitchen. I give you fifteen minutes," Kaitlyn commands.

Of course I follow. So in the next fifteen minutes I take the ham out of the oven and throw it somewhere outside, so the birds will have a little something to eat. There's always the classic Christmas meal of leftovers from the night before. So I open the fridge and warm up some nice pieces of pizza to go with the mashed potatoes and stuffing; I had yet to turn on the stove.

When I bring the food out onto the table, Kaitlyn is sitting there with the table and room looking completely like it did prior to the little flame incident. Well, excepting the nice artificial snow at our feet, the room looks pretty much the same.

I didn't realize how beautiful she looked when she came in. I always love a good Christmas dress. I think I could get used to eating at a table with her. If only she would see things the same. Well maybe after a little bit of wine she'll change her mind.

PART III

My brother and I were close, well as close as we could be. He would always try to act superior in his accomplish of age, but this is only expected. Looking back now, it kind of makes me smile. Look who's standing now!

But then I remember the things I miss. I mean, it's not like these things would be able to have been kept up anyways; life carries us on and on. That makes me frown. Now I'm left standing.

It's those memories that really change how you look back. Those times that I did something totally different then was in my normal were the moments that brought me closer to those spirits dancing in the back of my head now. My brother and I held those, those little spirits together that just sparked when put together. Perhaps it was the combination of our genealogy and just that boyish presence that kept us up.

We'd spend countless nights creeping from one room to the other, as to not wake the sleeping watchers on the couch. And in these moments, we would share that brotherly bond. It's something that even death itself cannot shed.

Sure we spent many nights together talking, reading, telling stories, all those boyish things. The usual sad result was mom and dad walking in on my brother and me the next morning as we slept peacefully head to toes on the bed. Sure his feet stank, but a pillow would always take care of that. It was a vigilant sacrifice well made.

There was one night that was just perfect. We both knew right away that it was the perfect setting. Well past midnight, we would peak out at each other and just nod in agreement. I think the best thing was the rain. Soon after I made the covert hop to his room, a huge thunderstorm kicked in and drowned out any noise coming from the room. We stayed up that night and talked and talked and talked about things that young boys shouldn't really talk about but needed to talk about as just a part of that inner male curse that makes us who we are.

Ah yes what a great time we shared that night! It was one of the last times it ever happened, like one of the last times we got to have that great bond as the lightening flickered through the window. It was one of the last times our parents got to act like they didn't know what was going on.

Soon after, letters would take people away, and letters would make others suffer with a burden that gave chance to the spirits, only to flake away.

I got a letter in the mail today. Apparently I'm still in some database in the school system (surprise, surprise). I don't see how else I'd be invited to attend some volunteer thing at the hospital. The letter was very attractive; it showed lots of people in hospital beds talking to the young adults of ten years ago. Everyone is smiling and cheery. I don't see why I can't go and find out.

So I hop in my car and take the fifteen minute drive to the hospital. Hopefully I won't ever have to come by another mode of transportation. Who knows?

The building's pretty new. I'd say built within the last five years. I'm surprised to see it so well constructed in today's society of medical attention. I park off to the side and take a short walk through the sliding glass door into one small room, and then another sliding glass door into the reception area. I guess it's also the front desk (hence the big desk in the front) and a waiting room (hence the families waiting around in the room).

I approach the pretty little Chinese woman at the desk.

"Can I help you?" she asks prettily.

"Yes, I hope. I'm here for the volunteer program thing," I reply.

"Oh! The Student Exchange Program for the Betterment of our World (SEPBW, Copyright 2007 All Rights Reserved, Job Six Months plus...)" and she lists off a bunch of pretty different things about the program that I translate to "blah," well a pretty "blah."

"Sure, that's the one."

And so she stands up and moves prettily to some files off to the left and prettily picks up the prettiest of all and opens it up, prettily.

"Here you go. You'll be talking to a patient to keep them entertained. Hmm..." she looks at me up and down, "we'll give you the one in room 125. It's right down the hall to the left there and then down at the end. Follow the signs if you get lost. Remember that's room 125. Oh! And my name's Sue."

She puts out her pretty hand and offers a shake. I grab it, flip it to backhand up and kiss it. She blushes. I smile and walk down the aisle.

Off to room 125 I go. Down the hallway to the left past room 119, where a man lies in his bed with a tube down his throat, past room 121, where a stern man sits off the side of his bed looking out, past room 123, where a man has fallen asleep in the middle of scratching his face, and finally to room 125, where my conversation piece awaits me.

"Who the hell are you?" a little old lady asks as she stares at me standing in the doorway.

"Me? I'm just here to talk to you. It's some volunteer program thing. My name is–"

"Oh, I'm sorry, I thought you were just another one of these nurse people coming to wake me up. Here shut the door. They keep you locked up in here like you've done something bad. I swear if I get one more shot in my ass I'm going to get up…" she struggles to sit up in the bed, then gives up and lays down, "…and, and…oh never mind."

"Well, what's your name, my name is–"

"Stop kid. Look, you look real nice, but I'd rather not do the whole name exchange thing. One less person to worry about, and then you don't have to worry about me."

"Alright, if that's what you want. So what do you want to talk about?" I ask her politely.

"Oh shit, I don't know. First go and get me a Diet Dr. Pepper. Here, there's fifty cents sitting in my purse there. Don't take any more."

"Alright, I won't. Where's the machine?"

"It's back out in the lobby. Don't come back until you get what I want," she states smiling. It's cute how the little wrinkles around her lips show a sense of gratitude yet urgency for her desires.

And so I walk out as ordered and go back past the rooms down the hallway and into the lobby where my mission lies, to checkpoint C where the soda machine sits. Fifty cents a pop, now there's a good deal.

And back past the pretty lady at the front. She smiles prettily as I go by.

And again past room 119, where the man still lies with a tube down his throat, past room 121, where the stern man still sits looking out the door, past room 123, where the sleeping man has frozen pointing straight up into the sky, and into room 125 where the little old lady lays in her bed.

"Ah! You did it. Good job kid. Thank you. You're too kind," she states as I enter.

"Don't mention it."

"So tell me kid. Why are you really here?" she asks expecting something.

"What do you mean?"

"Well, did someone force you to come? I bet they did. Ha! Tell me!"

"Huh?" suddenly there's a slow glow from the heart monitor as two emerging eyes take shape, glaring down upon me.

"Tell me kid! Your parents make you come…"

And her voice fades out and the eyes take over. They're staring down, down upon me, watching my every move. So blue are they, yet there is no beauty anymore. They have lost that touch of life, that spark of freedom, that link of hope. They have lost time.

When I finally returned home after running about and searching for something I could not find, I realized just how tired and worn out I was. The whole time, this single thought never even passed my mind. I was blocked from that feeling.

I walked through the front door; it was still open. This time I shut the door behind me, however it still felt as if I was outside. While I was away, the cold had lingered into my home, slowly filling every room. By the time I had returned, freezing air sat idle in every room. I kept moving to keep warm.

I paced randomly about the house, until I heard the dial tone above the normal electronic buzz a house entails. The phone. I hadn't heard it the entire time I had returned home, but then again I was only slowly regaining my feeling. My senses had been numbed by night's harsh breath. My ears popped, and the tone grew louder in a split second.

I walked into the kitchen and stopped in my tracks. A few hours ago this phone had given me the news. The news that ultimately changed my life. I hated it for that. I regained my composure and slammed the phone onto its base to hang it up and stop that horrible noise. I turned my back on the phone and took three steps, until I realized the tone was still there. It was growing louder and louder. I walked hurriedly into my bedroom to rid myself of this annoyance. I slammed my door.

It disappeared. It had gone away. I heard the tone no more. What have I done? I had just cut the very last tie I would ever have. I had been tied to a rope to suspend a boulder hanging over a cliff, and I had cheated. I had grabbed my knife and cut myself loose of this boulder. I heard no crash though. It never hit the ground. I was falling alone.

I had to regain its weight, so I reopened the door, but I still heard no sound. No sound at all. Not even the normal electrical buzz a house entails. It was all gone. I was not deaf, for I could hear my own pattered breaths echo throughout the house, but that was it. Myself. The noise I made was all that was left.

My power had gone out. I was alone in my room with no one to talk to. No one left to see. No one to hear my prayer. There were no words left to say. Then it hit me.

A tear formed down in my stomach and slowly protruded itself to my eye. Another soon followed. Before I knew it, I was choking on my own absence of breath. As I heaved and choked on the carbon gasses, my head began to float away. In whatever consciousness I had left, I moved towards my bed. I didn't make it.

I didn't sleep that night; nor was I ever awake. I hadn't passed out either. I just didn't have any control over my body. Each time I'd roll over on the carpet, I could feel the cold soaked stain from the previous hour's worth of tears.

When I originally received the police report, I didn't know what to make of it. It read:

"At approximately 12:37 AM on Highway 90, a black Ford car crashed into a silver Saturn pickup. There was one driver in the car and the pickup had a driver and two passengers, a family. The driver of the car was driving in the wrong lane and without his lights. At the top of a hill, close to the intersection with Edenfield Road, the car failed to change lanes and smashed head on with the pickup. The male driver of the pickup was killed instantly as was the male driver of the car. The female passenger of the pickup was killed as her airbag exploded. The younger adult male passenger was thrown through the front windshield from the backseat, as his seatbelt had failed to hold. Both vehicles were totaled. Initial reports of toxicity levels of the drivers show the driver of the car to be over the legal limit of alcohol. Report of this accident was called in by a local homeowner, Robert Shawler. Mr. Shawler witnessed the accident through his house window, but, being in a wheelchair, he was unable to act himself…"

And this went on and on and on, detailing every single action taken by the police. It still doesn't matter, they are dead. All of them are dead.

With this, it still pains me to think of the buzz of electronics. This modern day and age has failed. Technology has failed. Everything made to stop and help has only contributed more. This is the last draw.

With ever single bit of anger boiled up inside me, I shift with a controlled pace to the garage to find the tool I will need. There sitting in the very corner of the absent space in the garage is a baseball bat, my tool. I grab it and walk swiftly to my computer. I stand and stare at it. It is just sitting there. Sitting and mocking. It is mocking everything I have thought it stands for, every tie I had made to it. Just sitting there. The black screen staring back at me as I gaze under my eyebrows. It hums with the slow current of electricity. No more.

With one swift lift of the bat, I drive it straight into its glass face. Who's mocking who now? The shatter sends pieces flying everywhere. It isn't enough for me. I need more. More pain for this monster conspirator. I smash it again. A spark flies. Damn you Satan's hand! I swing again. The monitor stops humming.

It still isn't enough. I have only destroyed its face. I have to tear its heart from its place. It deserves to live no more. I have to make it bleed! I need to cut it up. I need to see the heart fulminate. I swing for the tower unit. The dust of metal, glass, and plastic stick to my face.

Every bit needs to be annihilated. I go back and forth from printer to tower to monitor to speakers to keyboard and mouse -- everything is against me. I have to remove it from mind. I need to erase the pain.

As I swing wildly around, I bite back the tears forming in my eyes. I stop in the middle of the room and view the damage. Shards of broken metal and glass are at my feet. I have cuts on my legs; blood drips to the floor. A single tear forms and drips down the side of my face.

I can't let it get to me. Not this. Nothing more. Nothing more can get to me. I am emotionally untouchable. No more pain. No more hurt. No more of this. No more! I have to make one final move.

I take a step and feel the crunch of glass as it cuts into my foot. I take another step. The power cords of the computer have been left untouched. There is only one way to finally rid myself of this demolished machine: I have to take its power away. I knell down and reach for the power strip. I remove each cord from its socket one at a time. Each time there is a spark, and a humming noise dissipates. Five cords. Four cords. Three. Two. One. One final cord to go. One final link. One last chance. I can't let it have that.

I reach my hand over the warm plastic and grip tightly. One last thing to do. As I pull the cord out of the socket, a jolt springs through my body and sends me plummeting across the room, on to all the shards of plastic, metal, and glass.

I eventually wake up, but I feel no pain, or so I think. I sit up and feel the rush to my head. Back down I go. The next time I come to, I stay down and crawl into the living room, leaving a blood trail along the way. I sit there for a little bit thinking about what I have just done.

It doesn't really matter. I can always buy another computer.

My father worked for this big company. It was something that did something for someone, so that they could do something for someone else, ultimately landing money back to the first something. I'm not really sure what exactly he did, but he brought home enough to pay the bills. They always told me this was a good thing. I guess it's true -- I like to have hot water when I shower too.

My dad would always wake up at like six in the morning, go to work, work, eat lunch, work more, go to the bathroom, work again, talk to the boss, work into the night, come home. This was his routine that he followed every single day. It's no wonder why over the years he slowly expanded in a, well, fat kind of way. There was a time when my dad could fit into a size 40 R tux, the one they gave to me before the accident, the one I wore at the funeral.

When dad would come home at night, he'd mumble and groan to himself, never letting it show though when the kids talked to him. It's one of the things I respect him for; I never even could grasp how what he did was hard. I mean, he only went to some building and then came home. Never sounded that exciting to me. So I made stuff up, stories, secrets, conspiracies.

My father was in the CIA. Now this isn't actually true, but it's one of the things I was most sure of while growing up. How could you go to school every day for so long and then just end up living a life of unpleasant circumstances? I could never imagine myself throwing my life away, so my dad worked for the CIA.

He always traveled during the week, all over the world too. One day he'd be in Oregon, the next in New York, DC, Europe, and then home again. It was a sporadic pattern of away and home. Somehow he managed to balance his work with his family. My mom always told me the dangers of working in some government agency.

She said, "Lots of people end up having their families leave them because they're never around. Just think about it for a little while, ok?"

I suppose I just never got the last part of those comments, because I never did put another thought to it. If my dad can do it, I can do it and more. It was the family shoes to fill. Someone had to do it. Someone had to take the responsibility for this country. I would follow in that path. I would be the one to protect the world. I guess you could say I had high dreams, but they were only dreams.

None of this was true, well, most of it was false. My dad did travel a lot for his job. I guess that's what got them into the situation they were put in. That's how they were driving home. That's how my mom, dad, and brother were coming home that night, that morning. Thirty-two minutes into the day. They new day. The new day for the world. The new day that would only last them thirty-two minutes. Thirty-two minutes just doesn't seem to compare to the amount of time I never got to spend with them. Neither does money make up for that loss.

I received some ridiculous amount of money. It came from various sources. The driver of the other car, my dad's company, and lots of legal things I didn't bother sticking my head into. I was consumed with other things. My mind was eating up the world I had left and savoring every bite, every drink.

It's Friday. A perfect February night. I'm not really sure what makes anything perfect, but this is perfect. I can feel it. There's something in my blood that's just warming, and it's a nice feeling. The telephone rings.

"Yello!" I say in mood.

"Get ready for a night out with me."

It's Kaitlyn. She sounds excited.

"Ok I will. When and where?"

The phone is dead.

Well that's real nice of her. She calls me, tells me what to do, and then hangs up. What a friendship.

There's a knock at the door.

"Coming!" I yell.

I walk to and open up the door. It's Kaitlyn.

"You just called me. What do you want?" I ask.

"Why aren't you ready?" she looks at me as though five seconds was plenty of time to get ready.

"What makes you think I'm not ready, huh? I'm always ready!"

"You don't have any pants on," Kaitlyn points out.

"Oh."

I go into my room as Kaitlyn comes and sits on the couch. I take five minutes to get ready, as she flips through the television.

"Anything good on?" I ask.

She shuts off the television.

"It doesn't matter, because I have a surprise for you."

"Ok. Sounds like fun. Any chance of finding out what it is?"

"I said a surprise." She looks at me with her mouth locked and the key thrown away.

"Ok. I'm all yours. Let's go."

"Are you sure you're ready?"

"YES!"

She looks at me.

"Why do you ask?" I say.

"You don't have any shoes on. Have you been drinking today already?"

"Only a little. And maybe I don't want to wear shoes. Kaitlyn, are they really that important?"

"I guess not. Let's go."

We walk to the front door. There's a splash from the fish aquariums. I turn back.

"Don't worry about it," she begs.

"Just a second. I…I don't think I've fed them today."

I go back over to the aquariums and drop some food in the water. There's no sign of the fish, the beast, but then again, there's no lights on. I push the black button and the bulb flashes brightly, flickers for a moment and then dies. I pause a second. Did I really just see what I thought I saw? That fish was huge! It must have doubled its size since the last time I saw it. My! Well, no need to worry about the burnt-out bulb now.

"Let's go!" Kaitlyn yells after me.

"Fine," I mutter under my breath.

She drives me somewhere. I'm not sure where, she made me keep my face looking down the whole time. She likes surprises, even more when she's in control of them.

"Can I look up now? My feet are getting awfully boring to look at."

"Go ahead and look, but this isn't the surprise."

I look up. It's absolutely beautiful. There's this great big oak tree covered with Spanish moss, and ivy is growing all up and down its trunk -- utterly breathtaking.

"So what's my surprise?" I plead.

She pulls out an object covered in a red velvet cloth. Gracefully she pulls the cloth off to reveal a bottle. One single bottle of whiskey.

"I found it in my house. It's from 1847. I thought you might want it...you know...for...you."

"Wow. Kaitlyn, this is too much. I can't accept this."

She gives me a look and shoots that down.

"That's very nice of you," I change.

I peer up at her and say, "Thank you. Do you want to try it?"

"No. That's for you. I want you to enjoy it," she says.

There's a knock on the car window. A middle aged man is glaring down at us. I look at Kaitlyn and begin to get up. She grabs my arm and pulls me back down, looks at me and shakes her head, and then gets out of the car herself.

"Hi there. Can I help you?" she asks the man.

"What are you kids doing here?" he grunts.

"Nothing…" Kaitlyn starts.

"I don't like the look of this," the man says, referring to the bottle and to the fact that we are two people of the opposite sex in one car in the middle of some forest.

"Oh…"

"Do I need to call the police?" he threatens.

"Can I talk with you alone, please?" Kaitlyn asks.

"Sure, whatever," the man says as he pulls his jeans up.

Kaitlyn shuts the door and the sounds go dull. I can still hear what they're saying.

"Do you remember that accident that happened around here a little while ago with that one kid's family that was all killed?" Kaitlyn asks.

I wince.

"Yeah, I think I remember that," the man replies, "What about it?"

"Sir, we weren't doing anything, but that kid in the car there is the one that lost his family. He's been through a tough time. I was only trying to lighten his mood…and the alcohol was for…"

"I understand," the man says, "I lost my wife a little while back."

He began to walk toward me. I roll down my window.

"Son, I know what you're feeling right now. I went through the same thing when my wife died. Listen to me. It's ok to have a couple drinks, but you can't drink your life away because of this. You still have a chance to live on. Take advantage of that opportunity. You'll only drink yourself to death, and how does that make you any better then the man who hit your family?"

I'm shocked. He said all the right words, true words, but how could he? Who is he to give me advice? He doesn't know what I've been through. He doesn't know anything!

"Yeah, ok…" I mutter.

"Alright, now you kids get on home safely now," the man says as Kaitlyn gets into the car.

We drive off. I look down at my feet the whole way home. Kaitlyn and I don't say a single word.

The funeral:

It was a week after they died. Exactly seven days. Seven's a good number. I think it has something to do with the Jewish calendar, or maybe some lucky number. I heard once that it was originally "on cloud seven," but then Christianity took over and yadda yadda yadda...now it's "on cloud nine," like the song. Nine's a good number too, but it was seven days since their deaths.

Three bodies. Seven days. Twenty six letters in the alphabet. Altogether that comes to thirty-six, which leads to the number six. Six: the number of legs all insects have.

That's what I felt like, an insect. I felt like a little bug with six legs and two antennas. And the funny thing is, with all those sensory organs, I couldn't stand up. The voice of the priest echoed in the background.

"Brothers and Sisters: we are gathered here today to mourn the loss of some of our dearest loved ones..."

And during the entire sermon, there I was, crawling in the grass, searching for a flower to grab hold of.

"...Is there anyone present who would like to say a word?"

And then someone stepped on me, and I was smashed into the earth beneath my feet. I had to walk away. It must have looked quite sad to see the only descendent of a long line of kings and queens walk away from the newly laid thrones of earth and stone. It wasn't my fault. No, it was my fault. Even the crickets can choose to chirp.

I went out to the car. It was a black car. Very nice. Some man had donated it to the funeral agency, and they in turn used it to transport the family members of the deceased. I guess that's how it got the nickname as the "Sad-Cab." I didn't shed a tear.

Why would I shed a tear? There's nothing I could've done to stop it. There's nothing I could've done for my future. It was all messed up, set in stone. And the funny thing is, the stone had writing all over it, but no one could figure out what the different languages meant. They only recognized one of the languages. Perhaps someday some man could figure it out and tell me how to speak it.

I sat there in the car and spoke to no one. People came over afterward and knocked on the window. I guess they got the hint once I didn't respond. They moved on. I was looking at a spot on the back of one of the seats. It kind of looked like the state of Illinois, and in turn looked like Abraham Lincoln. Good ole' honest Abe! What would our nation due without a man who stuffed secrets in his hat.

Since then, I've always meant to get one of those hats. I think it'd be nice to have a nice big hat that only you can get to. Imagine it. Someone asks if you have that on documentation or if you still have your receipt for an item you are returning, and then you say, "Why yes! Yes I do!" pull it out of your hat and voila: you have everything you could ever need. Still doesn't stop you from making bad decisions, but hey, at least it's stylish.

Some man came into the car and drove me home. I went to sleep. That's the extent of the funeral. No party for their entrance into heaven, at least not with me around. No toasting to moving on. But that's not to say there wasn't some toasting to myself, to freedom and liberty. I could finally buy that hat.

And so I place that hat on my head for a little spin around the old melting pot of the witches stew; it's another party. Parties are always interesting. They are always the same pattern of rhythmic dreams bouncing about across a wild page of weather torn.

I'm driving now to the so called "Biggest Blowout of the Year" (thanks to the absence of some neglecting parents). I swear, if I ever have kids, I am going to have video cameras in the house, so that I can see everything my child does while I'm out. On second thought, I might not want to know what happens. I don't think I'll have kids though, so it really doesn't matter.

The only thing that is of importance is getting to the correct location at the right time to be shuttled to the house of wondrous waters. The person whose parents are out, a girl, somewhere around 17 or 18, doesn't really matter, wants everyone to park in a specific joint by her house, just in case her neighbors are watching -- paranoia really gets the best of people sometimes, but whatever, I don't really care. After parking at the LZ, we'll be shuttled to the house, upon which the party may commence.

I arrive at the LZ at around 7 PM. The girl whose name I honestly cannot tell drives up in a small car. There's about five people waiting, two of them seem to be friends, but no one else seems to associate with each other.

"Hey, Kaitlyn told me about this and said it'd be cool if I came."

"Yeah, sure, have fun!" it's obvious she's heard of me.

There was a questioning look at first, and then at the mention of Kaitlyn's name, she nodded as if to not care for any other information. Whatever, I still get to go to the party.

We arrive at the girl's house, about five minutes away from the LZ (an abandoned pizza joint), and unload quickly into her house. It's obvious she's gotten this down to a science. The neighbors must not see anything! The only way the neighbors wouldn't be able to tell is if they lived a mile apart and had difficulty with vision and hearing, preferably above the legal age of senior citizen. None of the options were favorable to secrecy. Whatever, it's not my house.

There are about fifteen people inside, and everyone is making small talk. Amongst the midst of chatter, I hear a rumor that no one is allowed to drink until later, somewhere around 10 PM. As I continue to circulate, I get a better view of the crowd I'll be spending the night with. There's a couple on the couch, all over each other.

If I had a ruler, I'd need to slice it with a titanium razor to get a measurement of their proximity. There's a larger group of people, friends from some sort of group.

"Hey you!"

"Me?" I reply.

In front of me is a unique girl, not pretty, but not ugly. Beauty seems to be something she puts on with makeup. Her tone is snappy and her brows sharp.

"Do you know if Kaitlyn is coming?" she asks.

"No, she just told me about this. She didn't tell me anything else."

"Oh, um, thanks."

She filters back into the crowd. I look around and see a cup. It definitely has alcohol in it. The person holding it is already acting too loose and causing quite a loud ruckus. Either that or they're just normally a loud obnoxious bitch. Whatever.

The girl whose house we're at approaches me a motions for me to move in the other room. We walk into what I assume to be her room, and she shuts the door.

"Look, Kaitlyn told me about you."

"She did?" I reply acting surprised.

"Yeah, she said that you're usually good at being responsible and stuff."

"Yeah, right, sure I am. If you want me to do something…"

I have a feeling at what she's getting at.

"Well, I was wondering if you wouldn't mind holding back a little on the alcohol until later. I have a friend coming at around 11, and I need someone to pick her up. You wouldn't mind, would you?"

She expects me to deny her request. It's obvious that her normal friends would look at her and say, "Hell No!"

"Sure, that's fine. Do you think I can just go ahead and go to where we all parked? I don't want to destroy the party by being the only sober one…"

"Yeah, here are my keys!" she says as she tosses me her loaded key-chain. "See you later tonight!"

"Yeah, later."

I move out of the room and back out through the lingering crowd and out into the garage. I hop in the girl's little car and open up the garage door, then I turn on the car (always after opening the garage door. I heard of someone dying, because they past out with their garage door shut and their car turned on. That'd be a peaceful way to die). I finally drive the five miles to wait at the LZ. I wonder whose coming.

When I park the car, I flip the windows down, the radio on, and my seat back. I got time to kill, so why not do just that. To the sounds of some echoing acoustic guitar, my eyes drown in burden. A little nap wouldn't be too bad…

The last time I remember music and my family being involved all at once, besides of course the traditional caroling of songs in the car, was at a bar in town. My dad was invited there by some friends he had made in some softball league for old men wanting to keep that youth.

They took it way too seriously. It just seems to me that if you're only out there to have fun, you wouldn't bad-mouth the umpire, spit on the opponents, yell nasty words in all directions, or do a combination of all three, but that's just my opinion. I understand the need to get that male hormone off, that need that drives the fights and speed when you realize your opponent can kick your ass. I do understand that. I just always found it interesting how a bunch of businessmen can turn from the "yes-sir" environment to the "What-The-Hell-Are-You-Blind" type offered on the field.

Anyways, so it was a family gathering at some local bar where a live band was playing. That was the first time I had beer. Nasty stuff it is. Bitter and dry and rough all in one sitting. It lacks class completely. It's honestly the American drink.

After the live band played, the old bearded man in the corner spun some CDs while all the men, women, and children sat around talking of current events and business. It was boring for us kids there, so we ran off outside to run around and be ourselves, young and immature with no mind for business.

Someone found a football and so a game was picked up. After about three plays, we young and immature kids broke out into a fight. Maybe it was the heightened senses due to the buzz of beer, or perhaps that natural male hormone, it doesn't matter. After beating each other up pretty well and bruised, my brother came out and saw what had happened.

"Oh, Dad is going to be so pissed!" he said as he just stared at me smiling.

I think he was a bit proud of me, but it was obvious he desired to see more pain towards me that night, so he ran inside to grab my parents.

"Wait. Don't!" I cried after him, but it was to no use.

Looking around at the bunch next to me, each and everyone equally bruised and battered, I decided to get a little sneaky.

"Hey, listen here's what we're going to," I said as everyone huddled around me.

When my brother ran out, he was in for quite the surprise. All of us kids had brought the game back up, and just as if it was planned, as my parents were walking out, I was helping a fallen player up.

On the way home, my brother sat next to me with a look of defeat but also with a new found sense of respect. I looked out the window. My mom and dad looked at each other, with my dad of course looking at the road the majority of the time.

Knock, knock, knock.

I open my eyes and there's a girl looking down at me. Oh yes, the party. I turn the car on and look up at her. She's beautiful, very beautiful.

"Umm...are you the one driving me to that party?" she asks timidly.

It's perfect, I have all the power to make the right moves.

"I don't know what party you're talking about, but if you hop in I'm sure we can find something to do."

I'm and idiot. I can't believe what I just said. The girl just sits there taken back.

"I don't know why I said that. Yeah. I'm the one. Hope on in," I say trying to recover, "I'm sorry."

"Umm...yeah. Just drive me please."

And so I drive her to where she wants to go. I would rather drive straight off a cliff, but any awkwardness can be settled with a little alcohol.

"Stop the car!" she says.

I see what she's talking about. There are cops at the house. She fumbles for her phone to call someone there.

"Trisha? It's Michelle. There's cops at the house. I don't know what you should do!"

She's panicking.

"There's nothing for you to worry about," I say.

"What are you talking about? There are cops at the house!"

"I know," I respond. "Look Michelle, just tell Trisha to tell whoever answers the door to not let the cops inside. They can't do anything unless they have a warrant."

"Really?" she says unbelievingly.

"Yes."

And so she relays the message to her friend. We park where we can see what's going on, but luckily the darkness doesn't allow us to be seen.

The cops walk up to the front door and knock. A girl who's smashed answers the door. After a quick exchange at the door, the cops walk to their car and drive to park outside the house, so they can still watch to see if anything is going on.

"Oh my God, it worked!" Michelle states amazed.

"We can't go there now. Not until the cops leave."

"Right. I agree. So where do you want to go?" she asks.

"Well, I figured we would just stay right here, if you don't mind. We can talk or sleep or whatever. We just need to be able to see when they leave," I tell her.

"Ok. Well, what do you want to talk about?" she asks.

"Tell me about yourself."

"Me? There's not much to know about me. You already know my name, Michelle. I have a mom and dad and live in my house with three sisters, I'm the youngest.

I guess I am basically your normal girl. I mean, I like girly things. Like this one time I was with a bunch of my friends in the mall and oh my gosh you would not believe it. We were just walking, and these guys came up to us and we all started talking. Well it turns out they were the costars of the chick-flick we were about to see, so we all went and watched it together and…you're not liking this are you?" she asks as my eye-brows are rising up.

"No. I mean, I said I wanted to hear about you. And I've learned a lot. It's a cool story. Really."

"Oh…well, sometimes I guess I talk too much, but hey, it happens. So what about you? Do you have any brothers or sisters?" she asks innocently.

"Yeah, I did…"

As the police flip off their car lights, there's a faint blue glow still radiating. It's cloudy but distinct. Like an eye just sitting there watching me, listening to me.

Everything around starts to spin as the eye grows closer and closer.

Blackness.

I've seen lots of flashing lights in my days. Too many. I remember in school being taught of the joy you should feel at the appearance of a cop, like it's a sign of safety. Lights are not that anymore. When you're driving down the road and sirens blow, you swerve off to the side to leave a way for the help. When you fall out of a tree and break a limb, you have someone dial 911 to come help you.

But it's painful when they have to come. I mean, the police coming to arrest you is one scary thing, but the ambulance is something else. It's painfully sickening to me. I guess it's just a trained gut feeling.

I was at the park with my brother one time, and we were climbing this huge tree. Honestly it's the biggest tree I have in my memory. With one giant trunk going up, it had roots reaching down from the branches that formed these little paths through the tree and also made it easy to climb.

About an hour into our little excursion, my brother turned to me.

"Do you hear that?" he said.

"What? What should I be listening for?"

"Sh! Just listen!"

Sure enough within three minutes, a fire truck and ambulance had arrived to come save us.

"Hello up there!" a man cried as he hopped out of the truck. "Is everything alright?"

My brother looked at me questioningly and replied, "Yes sir. Everything is just fine up here, is there a reason why you're here?"

"Oh, well the woman at that house on that hill over there called and said she heard some screams from the tree, like someone had fallen out," the fireman said.

"Well, I don't know what she was talking about, but we're just fine."

"Alright then. You boys be safe!" he said as he turned to leave.

"We will!" my brother cried out.

And as if that woman had the sense to tell the future, just as my brother's words echoed in my ears, I slipped off the branch and fell screaming down.

The next thing I remember was waking up in a hospital bed with a cast on my arm and my head pounding ever so hard. I never did meet that woman who saved me...or doomed me.

As my eyes slowly open up, I see a blurred spinning image of a womanly face. It's Kaitlyn.

"Kaitlyn? What happened? Where am I?" I ask her.

"Don't worry about it. Just get some rest," she replies.

"What happened?"

"Well, your friend Michelle called me when you passed out in the car. Luckily she didn't go to the cops, because she was stoned when I came and picked you up from the car."

"I need to get my car though," I say trying to sit up.

"Your car is here, don't worry about it. You just rest for now. Maybe we'll go see a doctor or something."

"No, I'm fine. I don't need a doctor. I just need to come around and sit up for a little bit."

Kaitlyn nods okay.

And so I sit up and spin around a little bit. Once I gain control, I tell Kaitlyn what happened.

"Lately strange things have been happening. I don't know how to explain it, but this isn't the first time this has happened. I don't know. It's just...I need a drink."

Kaitlyn goes to the kitchen and hands me some water.

"No. You know what I mean. I need a real drink. I just need to calm down a little bit, you know?"

"No, I don't know. I'm scared for you. I am," she says as she backs away a little.

"Could I just have my drink? Get yourself one while you're at it too."

"Fine, I'll get you a drink," she says as she goes to the kitchen to mix something up, "but I can't have a drink with you right now. I have some place to be."

"Oh, come on. Where can you go now? Just hang over for a little while."

"Look, I have school right now, and I don't know how I'm going to explain this one. Do you want me to just walk right into the principal's office and tell them that their ex-student has become and alcoholic, and I've been attending to that!"

She's serious.

"Oh wow, it's Monday. Hmm…Kaitlyn. Don't worry about me. Get back to class."

"You don't even remember Sunday. Dear God! I came over here and you wanted a drink. So we drank a little. No, I drank a little. You drank a lot! I understand having a little to get your nerves calmed a little, but maybe it's time to…I don't know…maybe you should try something else."

I just look at her. She hands me a drink.

"Just be careful, okay? Can you do that for me? Look, I have to go. I'll come by again some time," she says as she walks out the door.

"Kaitlyn, wait."

She stops at the door and turns around.

"Thank you."

"You don't have to thank me."

And with that she shuts the door and drives off.

Home alone again. Life has truly become somewhat of a drag. I missed Sunday? How does that happen? Why couldn't I have missed Monday?

I don't really remember my last day of school. To me at the time, it was just another day of school, which says a lot for what it is. School was consistent. School was boring.

I remember doing the same thing every day. I remember waking up early, oh dear Lord was it early! I remember sleepily getting something for breakfast, a piece of bread of some stale cereal. I remember driving to school, almost passing out to sleep at every light. I remember going to my first class, then to my second one, and on and on until my last one, and then I just went home. That was a school day. It's no wonder I gave it up when I had the chance.

Sure there were things I missed at first, like those few teachers who really touched your brain. My biology teacher literally cut a hole in my head and touched my brain. His name was Dr. Lector.

I didn't do much for school. I didn't put in that much. I got passing grades, but a passing life wasn't good enough for me. So I got out of just passing day to day to week to year to life, and switched to drinking day to day to week to year...we'll see where I go from here. I think the part that scared me the most was when my tenth grade history teacher laid out the possibilities we could take in life.

"Okay class, listen up," she said in a southern accent. "You each have a choice you can make. Each choice leads to a path, and each path leads to a lifetime of opportunities. First, you can get a job right out of high school. You will not end up happy. Or, you can go to college for four years and get a degree. You might be happy with that. But, if you really want to make an impression on the world, go to college for six or eight or even ten years! I just know you would be happy then.

The more education you have, the more ability you have to make an impression on the ones around you."

It's stuck in my head ever since, the bullshit that is, everything past the first sentence. That teacher is always surprised when she doesn't have students return to visit her with PhD's and grand spellings of education. It's not like the educational system is even holding up that well. It's so flawed. Too bad there's no point in trying to make a change.

I did try once. I wrote this piece of satire for English class. The teacher brushed it off and said she didn't have time to read it. I thought it was good, so I submitted it as a letter to the editor in the newspaper, of course using a false identity and all. The funny thing is that it ended up as an article in the newspaper, Local and State:

Muh School Be Good Fuh Me

My schooling has done well for me. I have learned to be smart. You can think so? I am a good student; try muh best. I in good classes -- all honors! Muh GPA is high: 2.7. I play football and basketball. Muh school likes me. Muh school likes muh athletic ability. Muh school haz been good fuh me.

Muh school makes me safe, but I bring a gun just in case. Muh friends would back me up. They muh dogs. Don't nobody try an' cross us. We smart boys. We beat them up. Muh school got cameras. Keeps me from doin' nothin'. Must not be nuttin' goin' on den. Still brung a gun though. Yea, muh school make me safe.

Muh school be on muh side. Muh people is muh teachers an' those other people. Dey like me. Let me do stuff utha people can'd do. Muh school celebrates muh heritage. Make me feel gud. It be good to have a month, ch'know? It be all we need fuh our history. It be all muh people need. It's what we be. Muh school be on muh side.

Muh school got da support of da people above. Each school district got a smart person on da board. Dey reflect muh future. I be smart just likes dem; likes muh family. Muh famly be large. Dey more then just muh moms an' pops an' bro an' sis. Dey muh community. Dey a strong communidy. Dey go ta muh games an' likes ta celebrate muh wins. Dey support muh school.

Muh school be good fuh me. Dey made muh futra. Muh futra be good. I gonna play a professhunal. Dey tell me I could. I will. If not, I gots a job. I uh cook. I make food. I could move up ta cash regesta sumdey. Dat'd be nice. It all tanks tam uh school. Muh school be good fuh me.

~James E. Clanton, PhD

Let's just say there were some things I wasn't so secure about with the school system. I think the best part was when the teacher held it up to the class as an example of what you can do when you have a solid background of education. Aspire to be something!

Well it's been three days since I showered last. I can sense the ripeness growing more and more with each movement about my life. It's absolutely disgusting, but I absolutely love it. It's something that I don't get to experience that often, so I'm going to take advantage of the opportunity. It's fun when no one really knows who you are.

I think I'll go and grab a bite to eat from a little Chinese place in the middle of town. The little drive will do some good, plus it'll be nice to get out and do absolutely nothing with my molding self. Maybe Kaitlyn will want to come.

Ring. Ring. Ring.

"Hello?" she says whispering in desperation on the other line.

"Hey, do you think you'd like to go for a little Chinese?" I ask innocently.

"Are you kidding me? I'm in school right now! I thought we already went over this. Look I have to go."

Click.

Hmm, guess she really didn't want Chinese. Well I do. So I go alone.

In the car, I don't turn on the air conditioner. The fumes fill up quickly and musk away until my own senses of smell, taste, and sight get used to the burning odor from my own body. I wonder how people would deal with something like this back then.

I park the car and can already smell the grease coming from the stir-fry dishes. I'm surprised I still have my sense of smell. Perhaps my little experiment has some confounding variables.

I walk in the door, and a couple sitting up front immediately looks up at me and then away in horror with a pained look on their face. Well that's just rude, but it's also extremely comical to view. I smile and move on.

When I get to the front counter, I ask for sesame chicken and rice. The man just nods his head and looks down and moves away. After standing there for about five minutes, a little Chinese girl comes and rings me up, the entire time looking down at the floor, and then hands me my food.

Well surprisingly, I got my food without much of an outcry. Time to go home.

As I'm walking to go out, a familiar face catches my eye off to the side. There's a girl just sitting there chuckling to herself.

"Well, Michelle. It seems we've ran into each other again," I say politely and walk over in her direction.

She looks up at me and just chuckles. There's a fire burning in her eyes, but it's calming for her.

"Hey, it's you. So, you made it just fine out of that other thing the other night?" she asks me.

"Yeah. Just fine. No worries. So...aren't you supposed to be in school?"

"Huh? What are you, my mother? Yeah I am. Well, they say I am, but I don't think I am. You know?" she says confused.

"Three pigs in a blanket never made it to the circus, because each time one tried to go, he realized he had to drag the others along with him," I state seriously.

"Huh? Yeah man. Whatever."

I just look at her and smile and walk off. It's amazing how much you really don't know about people. The thing that gets me the most is the image people always put up, as to say "I'm not good enough, so here's what you probably want to see." To me, life isn't real without the beauty in truth, even when the truth is an ugly one.

My brother and I had quite a grasp on reality. In fact we would spend hours at a time discussing its opposite, after a while mom and dad would make us shut the television off and put the controllers down. We couldn't help it. We were kids. That's what kids do now.

Sure we played outside plenty, but those rainy days were perfect. We had an excuse to delve even more into the sacred art of hand-eye coordination.

"Can we play something with two people?" I'd ask as my brother would play some one player game I never got to lay my hands on at the time, because he was the one who bought it.

Now I'm not talking about one of those big fancy systems they have today that make life feel like an illusion when you turn the TV off. I'm talking about the classic regular Nintendo. Greatest system ever made. It still works today, though I haven't brought it out for quite a while. How do I know it works then? For some reason it's easier to have faith in those articles of the past, they just knew how to make machines that would last forever. It's rare to find something like that, and you certainly couldn't find it being made today.

After about an hour of nagging on my brother, my mom would either give him a look, or he would just get fed up himself, so he'd pop in something we both could play. Simple games like soccer or football or track were the things we'd play. The track game was our favorite. Mom and dad didn't mind it as much either, because you would actually get some exercise doing it. It was a pad with these circles to run on. As if by magic, the little man on the screen would run when you ran. Simple little things like that would keep us active for about an hour.

Then we'd get tired and have to play something sitting down, soccer normally. Mom and dad didn't mind this one that much either, because my brother and I were on the same team, so it would prevent those fights like those in track or football.

After three or so hours of this, our brains would be worked to a great mush, so we would run about the house doing mindless things. Mom and dad didn't like this that much. They'd then shove two books in our faces and tell us to go and read. We'd look up at them as if they were joking. After realizing they weren't, we'd go to my room or his and act like we were reading.

Habit makes most of the things we keep in the future. It's a habit for me to act like I'm reading, when instead I think on something else. Back then I'd rerun plays from the video games to see where I had done wrong.

"I though I had it there at the end, you know?" I said.

"It looked like you might have, but it was predictable, so we lost," he replied as if he had been thinking about it too.

"How are you so good?"

He smiled and blushed, then got serious.

"You just need to practice more. Practice everything in life and you get better at it. It's just like a sport or school. You have to practice and study to be good at something," he said.

"You just, you just never practice at it, and you're just plain good. I wish I had that."

"I practice more than you think. Sometimes the greatest thing you can do is make it look like you don't practice as much as you do. Once you get there, nothing can touch you, because you'll be so intimidating," he spoke of wisdom. "Take driving. You never see me drive, but I always seem to get better at it."

"That's because you drive all over the place with mom," I said breaking his streak.

"But if you didn't know that, see?" he asked.

"Yeah. Yeah. I think I do finally see."

I think I'll go for a drive. Yes. A little drive would be nice. Just a quick spin around town. I like to drive. There's something about it. I guess it's because I don't obey the law. I like to speed. I ignore those signs that sit on the side of my vision; they are unimportant to me. All I need is the feeling inside my gut. That feeling was only cringed once.

I was driving home on the interstate when my parents were still alive. It was a nice summer day. The sun was to my side. I had my sunglasses on. I was ready for a nice drive.

So there I was jamming out to some nice summer music (whatever this means…I guess music has its seasons too, I just can't recall what I was listening to) and I merge onto interstate. My white Honda and I picked up speed the best we could (she's not the fastest, but she gets me from point A to B). We merge into the left lane and pass some cars. And pass some more cars. Merge into the right lane because someone doesn't know how to drive and doesn't realize that you should stay in the right lane unless you are passing (I always drive in the left lane), and so I pass them in the right, and then move back over to the left.

It was such a nice day. I didn't even think of my speed. I normally speed anyway, but usually I'm more attentive and aware of my surroundings I guess. I would have to say it was the sun that distracted me.

I was about two or three hundred yards from my exit, when I looked up in my rear-view mirror, and there were the lights. It took me a second to process what I had seen.

"Shit."

That's all I could say. And as I slowed down, I pulled over on the side of the road, the place I had so much criticized of others. I was literally ten feet from my exit.

I put her in park and shut her off.

"Well, shit."

I knew what would be asked for, so I pulled out my license, registration, and insurance card. There was a knock on the window. I rolled it down.

"Officer?" I said, acting completely innocent, like I was shocked at being pulled over.

He didn't buy it.

"Yes I am. I'm Officer McCloud. Do you have any idea how fast you were going?"

"I thought I was going the speed limit, sir," I lied.

"Well, I've been following you since the 203," as if I know what that is, "and this is a 70 mph road."

"Yes sir. Is there a problem? I thought I was going that speed."

"Well, I got you going 96 in this 70 zone."

"Are you sure?" I asked, questioning my own stupidity.

"Yes. Uh, yes I'm sure. I'm going to need your license..."

I handed it all to him.

"Just wait right here," he said and then returned to his car.

I felt bad for lying to him. He seemed like a really nice guy.

"Well, shit. What are you going to do now? Mom is going to kill you. Dad is going to burn the remaining corpse. Just shit. I hope you've at least learned your lesson. Thank you mom. And now you're talking to yourself."

"Hey kid!"

The officer was at the window.

"Yes sir?"

"Alright, here's the deal. I just got called for an accident down the road, so I need to leave."

He looked off and then continued.

"This really isn't that big of a deal. Just don't speed. It's not safe…"

He continued to look off, unattached to his words.

"Basic deal. If I were to give you this ticket, it's four points on your record and a $187 fine. Just slow down son."

"Will do officer. Thank you."

And with that, he was off. My stomach was twisting for a while, but it soon calmed down. No ticket, no warning, just words. Words that I would put into action for quite a while -- at least until my parents' death.

So here I am now. Again speeding down interstate. Why not? No one is going to look after me now, so there's no parent to answer to. I speed because it gives me more control. I have more power on the road. I'm just a little more attentive to the side of the road now.

She and I are driving together still. I could get a newer car, but it wouldn't be better to me. This girl is what my parents got for me, so it's what I'm going to keep. We're close.

I pull off of interstate and slow down to a stop light. I'm the first in line. There's a man off to the side.

He holds a sign that reads, "Homeless and Hungry. Anything will Help." Why not? I've never done it before, so why not?

I stay looking forward at the stop light, but maneuver around and get my wallet out. Hmm. I have twelve dollars and a coupon to some donut place. How much do I give him? Enough for a meal, and why not throw in this coupon too; I'll never use it. I leave five dollars for myself and wrap the coupon around seven dollars.

What do I say to him? Something inspirational. Smile? That's nice. I'll look at him and say "smile," and then drive off. Like it really matters. He'll just go and spend it on booze and drugs and what not. It's probably a waste of money, but that's why I'll keep five for myself.

The light changes green. I pull up next to him and roll down my window. It's the first time I actually see him. He's covered in filth from head to toe. His raggedy clothes droop down over his shrunken bones. He has a yellow-stained beard that blends into his yellow-stained skin and reeks of hunger and pain. Well, we're all hungry and pained.

I hand him the money, but cannot find the words to form in my mouth. He moves his hand slowly and accepts it. He looks me in the eye and says in a shaky voice, "Thank you sir. God-bless you. God-bless you!"

"Mhm…I…"

I look off and drive away, leaving the man behind.

Four days after the funeral, I found myself sitting around my house. It was the first time I was really alone. Not just alone, like being by myself, but alone alone. It's the type of loneliness that hits with time, that loneliness elders feel when they sit in their house for years with only the occasional visit of a relative. I found myself sitting at the kitchen table, just sitting and contemplating nothing, because I really couldn't think.

My mind was blank (not that much has changed). I went to recall some memory, and all I could see was the faint whisper of a black screen. And in this black screen, there were black curtains that blocked out a black sun. The sky was black, the air was black; life was dead.

Then it just hit. This overwhelming since of loneliness, like Dostoevsky loneliness, without all the negativity (that would come in time), just hit and brought me to the brink of feeling something in my body. That slight trickle of a tight throat came over me, but it stopped at my eyes. My eyes were glossy, but no tears flowed. I sat there for an hour on the brink of tears, but I could not cry. I wanted to run again, but my legs were numb. I wanted to remember, but my mind was blank. I was blank.

Then came a knock at the door. I sat there a little while longer, hoping whoever was there would go away.

Perhaps I had a little spark left in my imagination, and there really was no one there.

Then came another knock at the door. I slowly rose and walked to the door and looked through the window. There was only a blur. I cracked the door open, hoping to appear uninviting. There stood a little woman. She was not old, but certainly not young. She appeared to be in her fifties, as shown by the worn wrinkles and wind beaten grey hair. She had a modest look on her face.

"Hi there. Do you mind if I come in?" she asked with a warming voice.

Without thinking I replied, "Are you the social worker?"

She looked off to the left and then back at me saying, "Yes. Yes. I'm the social worker. I'm here to talk to you about your situation."

"I'm sorry the house isn't more presentable. Here, step inside," I replied as if put in some trance by her voice.

She came in, and we moved to the table I had previously been stagnant at.

"How are you doing today?" she asked.

I just looked at her as if it should be obvious.

"Well, you certainly seem to be taking care of yourself so far. That will be the hardest thing, but you're off to a great start. I know it's early, but you need to start to look towards the future," she said.

"Shouldn't you have some type of papers for me to sign or something?" I questioned.

"No. Not today. Perhaps another day," she said as she stood.

She walked over to the counter and smelled some of the flowers that were sitting around. She then moved into the kitchen, looking around at every little detail, and then into the living room, and finally back to me. I just sat there and looked at the floor.

"Was this them?" she said, holding a picture of my forgotten family.

"Yes," I replied without looking up.

"They were very beautiful. It must be hard to have to let go of something like that."

"Yes," I replied, still looking at the floor.

She sighed and grabbed a chair and pulled it face on with me, well her face was looking at the top of my head, but she was in line with me.

"Look at me, please," she said.

"Okay," I said, raising my head up.

She had very beautiful eyes. They were a rich dark green, but something else was there. There was something else back in her mind.

"I'm going to be honest with you. You are very fortunate. While yes it's going to be hard to get on, I want you to look on the bright side. Think if this had happened later down the road. Think of all the more memories you would have with them. Think of all that waste! You are experiencing something like this at a very young age, yes, but you are also going to be given the opportunity to grow and learn with this. It is horrible what has happened to you, just horrible, but even so you must be strong. This will only make you a better person. In time you can move on and establish yourself. You must be the strong one. You must be the independent one. It's all up to you now," she said as a tear formed in her eye.

She stood to leave, and I sat there in disbelief. I didn't really know what she had said, but it made me feel different. Something about her words was so relating to me. It just all seemed to fit. It was horrible what had happened, but even so I must be strong.

As she opened the door, I turned to her and said, "Thank you."

She stopped halfway and collapsed a little. Several tears raced down her face, but they were quickly halted as she recomposed herself.

Breathing in and out, she said, "There's something I need to tell you. I don't want you to hate me, but I should be thanking you. I had to say that. Look, I'm not really a social worker. I just...I read about your situation in the newspaper. A month back I lost my mom and dad in a boating accident. I was an only child. And while it seems this old woman doesn't show it, I...I feel so much for you. I feel so sorry for you. Oh so sorry..."

Then she ran out the door bawling and left the door open behind. I sat there for a moment with an utter blank face. My eyes must have stayed locked on that door without blinking for thirty minutes. Then the wind came and blew the door shut.

It's at times like these that I find myself sitting alone in my house with nothing better to do than just that. And so here I am sitting on my bed in a time like this. In times like this, what better is there to do anyway?

Maybe I'll lie down.

"Okay."

Yes, I'm talking to myself. Too bad I'm not very good at a wide range of accents. I think talking to myself could be so much more interesting, if only I didn't sound so much like myself. Hmm.

I glance around the room, looking side to ceiling to side. It really gives a whole new perspective looking up to the world. I guess we all need to be humbled to sleep well at night. I know I feel better in the morning when I sleep laying on my back rather than sitting in some chair or, if God commanded, standing up. Must be me.

Side to my closet doors to my ceiling fan to my window. My door is closed. The lights are out. Night is only starting to stir in all its tranquility. Now there is something that we can't have! The night life should be interesting, should be throbbing with life. Sure there's life in the wind blowing through the trees, but where are the people. Where's that human quality that brings life out, that pounds it into your head harder and harder until a headache ensues? I guess sometimes the night has to rest too.

My window seems lonely. I open it.

"There, much better."

See what I mean? A nice German accent would sound great there.

"Window, it's too bad you have that screen there, otherwise I could pass right through you, and we could have a jolly good time frolicking through the night."

Hmm. I grab the tee-ball bat I keep next to my bed and pound it into the screen. It ricochets back and pounds me in the shin.

"Damn that hurt! Why'd you do that? Look, I understand that it can be painful to be jousted into like that, especially since you have no basis of experience in this area. Not saying that I'm an expert in something like this. Hell, I've never done anything like this. Do you think I'd go banging in like this if I knew what I was doing? This is the first time for me. This is the first time ever sneaking through my window. My parents would be so disappointed. I understand it's a bad choice, but I'm young, somewhat, and I have to live a little. I'll have to punish myself a little later, because God knows my parents can't. Maybe we should take things a little slower. I'll just...I'll just ease in with a knife and cut a little hole in the screen, and then maybe push in with my hand a little, and peel off all resistance to our escape! It's perfect. I'm glad we could come to this together. I'm glad we could do this together. It's nice to know you're here for me. It's nice to share some of my future with you."

And with that I hopped out the window, and made my escape into the night, but the window decided to stay behind and breathe a little. I understand. Things like that can be painful and breathtaking all at the same time. I know I have some scrapes and bruises from the experience.

Now the question lingers: how do I, a single man, liven up something as great as the night? There's only one way I can think of, usually the best approach to any problem. I'll just thrust my way in.

And so I run and run and run, until my lungs bang against my ribs and my heart pounds against my throat, and then I run some more. When I finally stop, I'm down the road quite some ways and making my way into town. Something is flashing…the nightlife?

No, it's a cop.

"Damn. Wait, I haven't done anything wrong, have I?"

I turn around, and the policeman gets out of his car, but stays behind the door.

"Why don't you come over here, so we can talk?" the officer demands.

"Is there a problem sir?"

"Well, for starters, it's three in the morning. Now what on earth is a kid like you doing out?" he says, expecting me to lie.

"Well, I just forced myself through my window and went for a little run," I replied calm and collected.

"And the reason for the scratches?" he asked.

"Oh," I blush, "I guess my window had something to say in reply."

"How old are you son?"

"Me? I'm...I'm an adult. I don't really know what day it is, so I could be 19. Most likely I'm still 18," I say unsure.

"Are you in school right now?"

I look across the street and see a man getting out of an old, beat-up car to get some gas. He's face looks strangely familiar. I know I've seen him somewhere. It's...it's the man, the homeless man on the side of the road, but he looks much younger and clean too. He's wearing an older suit, but one that holds a job. I smile.

"Hey son!" the cop yells, "I'm talking to you. School?"

"Oh, right, no. I don't go to school."

"And you're just out for a run then?" he asked disappointed.

"Right."

"Well, just be careful. You never know who's on these streets. Some homeless man could mug you or something," he says getting into his car.

He drives off in the opposite direction.

"No, there are worse men in this world then homeless men."

When I was about nine years old, my mom and dad started worrying about me. I could tell that they were, because every time I'd throw out some comment about certain people, they'd look sternly down upon me with absolute disgust.

"You know, I think that people who are homeless, I think it's all their fault. If they wanted to work, they could get a job," I'd say.

It was that transitional part of my life when I thought that everyone was in control of the world around them. I thought I had super powers. I could fly if I wanted or become invisible. Of course I never used them, but I knew if I needed to, they were there. I had control over this, why doesn't everyone have control of who they are?

About a week before Thanksgiving, my mom and dad approached my brother and me and said, "Boys, this Thanksgiving we're all going to do something different. We know that in the past we usually eat dinner together as a family, but this time it's going to be different. This year, we're all going to have dinner with many people that we don't know, but we are going to help them."

And with these simple words, we were off on Thanksgiving Day to go and help serve the homeless. My parents had volunteered us through some church organization in town.

When we arrived at the shelter, I was immediately fearful of what was going to happen. The outside of the building was enough to scare a little kid off. It was spray painted all over with gang signs and hatred smeared in blood. My brother and I looked at our parents and just stood there in shock.

"Come on boys," my dad said.

When we walked inside, a lady greeted us and asked us how she could help.

"No, we don't need your help, we're here to help," I said as my mom grabbed me and pulled me back.

"Sorry," she apologized for me, "we're here to help serve."

"Wonderful!" the lady said full of joy, "Believe it or not, you are the first to arrive. Thank you for your time."

We were taken to some back room and given some gloves and plastic caps, and then we went into the cafeteria to prepare for the feeding. I was on mashed potatoes, and my brother was on the stuffing.

One by one the people trickled in. Some were in families, but most were all alone. They walked down the line with their heads down in melancholy. Like drugged little puppies they walked by as I scooped up their desired serving. With each person, I watched a little of my ignorance fly away.

After an hour of serving hundreds of people, we sat down with some of the homeless at the end of the table and ate our meal.

"So why you here kid?" asked a man in a ruffled jacket.

"I'm here to help out..." I stumbled.

We had all sat there in silence for a while, so it had came as quite a shock when this man spoke to me.

"Really? You don't seem very happy to be helping out," he replied.

"I'm happy. Are you?" I asked.

"Kid, there ain't too much to be happy about these days, but yeah...I guess. This is a nice place. It's better then where I was before. But this ain't about me. I've lived a pretty good life. You just look sad. Why?" he asked.

"Huh? I'm not sad. It's just...everyone here seems so unfortunate. I just wish...I don't know..." I dragged off.

"Kid, look around. We all come from different places, but we all got something in common, you know? It's Thanksgiving. I ain't had that great of a life, but each day I pray for a little something more, and each day I get a little more. It's been a couple years since I've had a Thanksgiving meal like this."

"So, where are your friends and family?" I asked.

He looked down and said, "My wife, she uh...died with the kid in her. Got shot."

My parents looked at each other worried. The man saw this and nodded and moved on.

"But that was a long time ago. I got all the family I need right here. I got everything I could ever want right here," he said.

After the meal, we helped clean up, and then we drove home. The entire way home no one spoke. I think we had all had the experience affect us in a different way. Sometimes it's best to not say anything.

Have you ever had one of those moments? One of those moments when you're just sitting there and then... bam! Your life to come flashes before your eyes. It happened to me today. It was so...so real and so near that it felt like an alternate reality, like it wasn't me. It wasn't me, but it was.

I was taking a shower, and it just happened. I closed my eyes, and my future flashed before my eyes. I saw myself, in a blur, covered in something. I'm lying on the floor. It feels so cold. I was wet, no I am wet, no I will be wet. Maybe it was just the shower. But there's glass. That's what it is. I'm covered it glass. And...and my parents are looking down on me.

They were there, looking at me. Alive again and looking directly at me. I can't say what it was. They blinked and just looked. Stared constantly. Their eyes were so sad, so disappointed. What did they expect? Huh? I mean God damn-it they left me! Me! They left me alone with nothing. They left me with nothing!

And there was my brother, off to the distance, just looking at me with disgust. With pity. He might have well of just spit on me. How could he look at me like that? How could any of them look at me like that? Poor fools they are, what about me? Huh? What about the one they didn't take? What about the one God decided to kill more slowly? Why didn't you take me?

And that was it. No more. That was all there was in the future. But it's not true. They're dead. It can't be true. None of it can be true. Forget it. They'll never come back.

I get it now. They're gone. Every single one of them perished to a fire of a life that never was meant to be. A fire that burned out a long time ago. A fire that…that was never given enough wood to burn anyway.

I dried off and got out, never even finished cleaning myself. It wouldn't matter, I'd still feel disgusting.

One of the most impacting things that ever had an impact on my life was my graduation. It was the most beautiful sight to see. Filled with honor and distinction, we all smiled proudly as our parents watched from the cafeteria seats.

At the end of my fifth grade year, it was time to wave goodbye to those fond memories from elementary education. It was a day I know I will never forget. A stepping stone for my whole life.

Of course now I know that it wasn't much of an accomplishment, I mean, elementary education is such a laugh. Of course it is important for development, but life is full of development. People put so much pressure on kids back then. Everyone wanted their child to be the best. For them to be the one that got the straight A's. Of course grades are a joke. Even friends are a joke. No one really knows what they want back then.

I was friends with lots of people. At graduation, we all looked at each other with such ignorant eyes. Everyone was the astronaut, everyone the police, everyone the president. The greatest was the understanding of how the monetary system works.

Before we left school, our teacher presented us with a little problem.

"Okay class. I want you each to image that you had a hundred dollars. Now take out a sheet of paper and draw what you would buy."

And so I took out my sheet and drew a car. I looked to my left and that person had drawn a house.

"You can't buy a house with a hundred dollars. That must at least cost two hundred!" I said amazed at their stupidity.

The teacher heard this and came over.

"And you drew a car. Did you know that cars cost a lot more than a hundred dollars too?" she said.

Everyone in the class was humbled quickly at the pointing out of their ignorance.

And so on graduation day, we all smiled. We smiled in ignorance of what was to come. We were given these hats to wear and keep. They were baseball caps with our class year. How old we felt as we walked across the stage and received our printer paper. It made us dream of the places we'd go.

Of course, this wasn't the type of graduation that you'd send off announcements for, and so of course, no money would be sent back. It was a completely, introvertedly-inspired event. We felt good because of what we had done.

Six years. That's a lot of time. It took that much time to open up the Panama Canal. Think if that had never happened. We future six graders would be back under that little roof, sailing all around South America just to get to California.

So here it is. The moment everyone has been waiting for their entire life. It's this single moment that has driven over two hundred people to slack throughout a year, a year that I did not share a moment in. It is the day of graduation. I can sense the feelings of accomplishment in the air.

But what have I done? Why am I even going? Here I am cleaning up and throwing on a suit and tie, a nice black one with a red tie, and I'm going to help out at an event that I could care less to be at. I mean, sure Kaitlyn invited me, it's a big step for her, but for me it's just more dreams washed away into a storm drain that will go and be filtered out to be drank by someone else later.

I don't think I really want to go. I mean, why should I be put through more of the crap that I tried to steer clear of? It's nothing I need. I'm not getting a diploma. I'm not going to college. I'm not starting a life on my own. I already have a life that's filled of loneliness. Why would anyone want that? Why have all these people gone to school for that. I'm not going.

I press the seven on my phone and hold for it to dial.

"Hello?" Kaitlyn responds.

"It's me. I'm not going. I can't," I state hurriedly.

"Wait a second now. First, I know it's you. Second, what do you mean you're not going, I thought you said you'd help out. I thought you said you'd be there for me."

"I did, look, I just can't now. Why should I? I mean, there's nothing in it for me. That sounded selfish. Look I just --"

"If you don't want to go, then fine. It is selfish. I just thought you would be there for me," Kaitlyn says.

Click.

"Hello? Please, it's not that, look…"

She's not there. I can't go. If I go, it goes against everything. I just don't know if I can stand to see that. All the hats and robes and papers. The smiles and tears just seem like such a waste to me.

I tell myself I'm not going as I hop in the car and start to drive towards the auditorium. I'm not going. I'm not going. I'm not going.

I'm there. Damn. I can't even promise myself that I can hold it together.

I walk up to a little old lady whom I recognize from years past. She's the coordinator for the people passing out the programs.

"I'm here to help pass out to programs," I state as she looks at me.

"I know. Kaitlyn said you weren't coming. Hmm," she says, handing me some programs. "Here, take these. You'll pass these out over there at that door, one per person. After that, you may stay and watch if you'd like, and I'm thinking you should."

I stand there and look at her.

"Well, off you go," she commands and turns away.

Great. Glad to know what I'm to do. I guess sometimes it is better to know. What if she wouldn't have commanded me, I mean, what if I didn't have a chance at passing out programs? It's such a tedious task.

The doors open up and soon people start to poor in. I'm in the farthest door, so no one comes to me for a while. All the parents and friends go to the other volunteers, younger children from a grade down. I don't know how I got into this mess.

After passing out five programs, the lines die down, and people stop coming to anyone. Glad to know I could help. So I walk and take a seat in the back.

Slowly the ceremony takes place: speeches I care not to listen to, people I care not to look at, a place I care not to be in. And after all the bullshit stuff for face, the graduates are called up one by one until every last one of them has had there last moments of glory.

Kaitlyn walks across swiftly, she's ready to move on to a new world. How nice she looks in that robe with that awkwardly-shaped hat. Sure everyone looks nice, but she has a glow about her. I think I shall miss that. And off the stage she goes, back to her seat.

And as the final words are mottled, the hats go flying off with a future of dreams. It's over. It's finally over. But it's over. They're all gone. Kaitlyn is gone.

Somehow the mesh of people pulls me off and out into the open courtyard where smiling parents meet their newly graduated children. All of them so happy with tears of joy. Pictures fly left and right of friends and memories.

And there I am, standing in the middle of it all getting spun around and around as people move with the excitement of children on Christmas morning. It's all so cheery and so dark.

I don't know how to react. I can't smile. My eyebrows cringe in and I am filled with a feeling. A tear forms in my eye as Kaitlyn approaches me.

"You came!" she says from a distance.

I turn my back to her and slowly begin to walk away.

"Where are you going?" she calls as she tries to push through the crowd of happiness.

I duck off to the side and move away quickly and run to my car and drive straight home. It's a joy I do not hold. It's a dream I do not hold. It's a future I do not hold.

"As I sit and write this letter, I think upon my past. I think upon my present. I think upon my future. I am visiting these ghosts to sort things out, to sort out my virtues from my curses. I am writing this letter and posting it to my own address. In several days it will arrive back to whoever is here, and perhaps this is where we are at the moment, where you are at the moment. I do not know. I do not know where I have been. I am not that lucky. I do not know where I am at the moment. Sure my mind is influenced by many things, but influence leads to some path. I know not my path. I do not know where I am going. Somewhere. I will end up somewhere. We all do. I mean, we all end up somewhere eventually. I guess what separates the living from the dead is only a choice of where to end up in the future, for the dead usually stay dead, and the living usually end up dead. I understand this path now. And perhaps it is where my influences lead me. But regarding any future decisions, I urge you to take hue of this before making any premature assumptions.

In the past, my family is alive. My family lives in a home, everyone happy together. Sure we have our quarrels as any family does, but we understand it is the decisions out of these quarrels that define us, and so we do not judge each other with spoken words. In the past, my family eats dinner together. My mother and father love to cook. My brother and I look on with drooling anticipation. We always eat well, together as a family. In the past, my family travels together. We go to distant lands of wonder for all minds aged to youth. It is these places that keep us alive. It is these experiences that keep us desiring. It is these people that make us a family.

In the present, my family is dead. I stay in this house. I speak to no family, only an ugly image in a mirror of reflecting life. I eat alone, if I am lucky. I hate cooking. It is a waste of time. Food does not taste good anymore. All I do is watch it as it swims around on a cracked plate of hope and dreams. I eat poorly and drink worse. I am lucky to be able to stay inside. The outside world, when often ventured, becomes dangerous and hateful. I have no place to go, but no place to stay either. So instead of choosing one direction or the other, I sit. I mellow. I rot.

In the future, my family is alive. Someday we will have a greater home than many ever share together while living. Whether it is a home of clouds and sunshine or a home of dirt and darkness, we will have a light together. We will eat together, we will travel together, we will talk together, we will fight together, we will love together, we will hate together, we will hatch together, we will breathe together, we will play together, we will build together, we will grow together, we will will together, and we will live together!

And so for everything I hold in my life, I draw out these words on this paper. Perhaps they mean more to me than to you. Whoever you are, it does not matter. This is one thing you were unable to stop. This path that I have traveled, am traveling, and will travel is my own. I have fought beasts great and far, just as I am fighting now and will continue to fight. It is for many things I do so, but above all, I do so for my family. For my family will live together again."

Mickey Bahr

I cannot take it anymore. No more! Its burden has grown too large. No more can I feed the beast. No more can I fill its tank. No more can I look into its eyes! I must do something.

I launch myself out of my bed. The hallway does not spin. I am completely sober. I sprint toward the tank, stumble and trip over my own feet, and fall inches from its glass barrier.

I shoot my head up. My face is hard and my eyes unmoving from its eyes. I crawl slowly towards the tank, each movement burning my skin. I stop right at the glass. My nose touches. A soft ring of fog forms around my breath.

The beast holds still at the bottom. I wipe the fog away so it can see me. I touch my finger to the glass. Again and again, slowly stroking its cool surface.

The beast's whiskers seem to flare up. No more of this. No more!

I tap a little harder. The beast does not move.

Harder. Harder! My finger begins to hurt.

The beast shifts about the bottom.

Harder!

It splashes to the top.

I rear my fist back and crush into the glass. It cracks around my hand. Water slowly trickles out.

Yes.

Again I smash it and again! My hand goes right through, and the entire tank shatters free from its holdings. My hand gushes out blood. The water bursts out and fills the carpet around.

Where is the beast? It isn't in the tank.

I get to my knees and glance wildly around. My breathing is out of control. I cough hard and fall to the floor.

The beast is right there.

I glance at it. For a second it does not move, its whiskers held tight into the air. I blow on it. The beast begins to flap wildly about.

No.

No more of this!

I throw my hand on top of it, cupping its body. Something cuts into my hand. I yank it away and the beast sits there, gills moving in and out, grasping for air.

Yes.

My eyes begin to twitch and I raise my hand up slowly. I stop breathing.

In one swift motion I bang my hand down on top of the beast. It stops breathing. I raise it again and crush down, the bones crunch beneath my fist. I grin wildly. Over and over I smash the beast until it is gone from my mind.

I cannot get it out. I back away slowly and crawl to a dry part of the carpet.

I know what I have done. I have done it on purpose -- yes! I do know what I have done, but I know not why.

What has driven my hand to the glass? What has driven my fist to its still body? Why have I killed the beast?

I must call her. I must call Kaitlyn.

I scramble across the house to grab my phone, panting along the way. I reach my room and toss about looking for the foreign object. As soon as I find it, I hold hard on the number seven. It dials. She picks up.

"Hello?"

I want to speak, but my mouth allows no words. I groan.

"Hello?" she repeats.

She's still there. I throw myself into a coughing fury and hurl about my room, knocking over my lamp. The bulb shatters into my golden forest. I stand on the glass and the shards cut into my feet. I pace across the room as the blood leaves my trail.

"Is everything alright?" she asks.

"Of course," I lie.

After calming, I decide not to talk about anything. I do not mention the glass. I say nothing about my beast. I have found no reason.

"Hey, so I was reading this article earlier today and it said that…"

"Hey, Kaitlyn, I need to go."

"Okay…"

She's unsure.

"Are you sure everything is alright?" she asks.

I only mutter the simplest phrase.

"Acta Est Fabula."

The play is over.

Thus ends the last phone call I will make. I set my phone down, distancing myself from the contraption. I slowly move toward the living room to lie with the corpse.

It smells retched, but my nostrils will not process it. I won't let myself. Still, the taste lingers on my tongue.

As I lie, the water soaks into my clothing, chilling my heart. The glass cuts deep into my skin, but I feel nothing. As my blood mingles to the beast, I begin to think.

What has driven this? How does it end like this? I had conquered my beast -- this beast!

But after all, I will not allow myself to leave its side. The hands have already been turned, and now it is time for me to take my final action. I roll over on my side and glare into its eyes. Those blue-clouded diamonds meet my deep-set brown. We will never leave our glare.

I inhale.

With one final thought, I breathe all my life out, everything left for me. Every memory, every twitch, every time I dreamed left in that sigh.

I hold as my heart slows.

I hold through the soothing pain as my muscles twitch.

I hold as my eyes cloud over.

I hold as the blackness overtakes our glare…

They, those of experience, say your life flashes before your eyes right before you die. And as much as this cliché rings some truth, what defines your life? Is it what you did while here? Where you went? What you saw?

I see myself blind again. I'm curled up. It's pleasant, and I can hear laughter. I'm not breathing, but I'm alive. It's so soothing. I'll just lie here and sleep. There's no need to kick and shove about. I'm comfortable.

Wait, something happened. A jolt. I'm moving. They're moving. What's going on? We're in a car. I hear the keys hit the ignition. A voice. It's my dad. He's talking to my mom.

"It'll be okay, we're almost there. Just hold on a little bit longer."

And my brother. He's there too.

"Mom, are you going to be okay?" I hear him ask.

"I'll be fine dear. I've done this before."

It's my mom. She's speaking. God she has the voice of an angel. I don't know why, but I am so happy. They are happy. Despite the tension of the situation, there's a hidden joy deep within.

We're moving again. Going somewhere. Mom is in a wheelchair. I hear the wheels gliding across the floor. They're pushing her to a room. She's on a bed now. There's a doctor and some nurses. What's going on? Everything is spinning around. My view is smeared with a dizzying blur. Spinning slowly. Spinning, spinning, spinning…

I strain to open my eyes against the unknown force. I'm wet and I feel disgusting, but there's a sign of relief. Yes. There they are, looking at me from above. And there's my brother. He's off in the distance. He's laughing, but he has a hint of jealousy on his face. Must be the attention I'm getting from mom and dad.

They're not moving. None of them are moving. They're just sitting there, smiling. I'm smiling with them.

I shift my body up and feel a crunch.

There's glass. I look around. I'm at home. I look up and they're still there, smiling down upon me. A picture. A photograph in a wooden frame. But in pictures, there are people too. There are memories, stories, tears, love. There is a family. A family that is still there. A family that will always be there, with you, for you.

What have I done? Why have I lived like this? What has driven me to this point? So much waste, so much gone, left to the past…what is there for the future?

Most would consider it an accomplishment to tame a beast. Whatever its size, whether it's a snake or a dragon, beasts are wild creatures. They roam in the depths of darkness, lurching around for anything to harm. In a bottle of purified water, even today there are bacteria destined to make you sick. In the streets and down the alleys rapists and murderers sit, waiting for anyone to step in. Hurricanes flood cities, starting fires that burn the flesh of bodies later to just float around aimlessly.

Every building has its breaking point. Every rapist and murderer must evade the police. No matter how much you boil water, some disease always remains.

These are beasts, impossible to tame and altogether inconceivable to hinder growth. The beasts that roam in the depths of darkness are what cause fear and hysteria among many. They can try to stop a beast, but it only consumes their soul. It is a wasted effort.

These are the fools: they have not learned from the past; they repeat the mistakes of the past; they make themselves an item of the past. All the while, their beast lives on.

I have found my beast.

And there it is. I look at the lifeless fish sitting next to me. It truly is sad, because I feel some of my life went with it. Its eyes are wide open, glaring right back into mine like always before, but this time I feel no attraction. They're no longer cloudy. They're just blue. Blue eyes. Blue eyes on a fish. It's just a fish.

I strain to rise up and feel the jolts of pain from the cuts and scrapes that cover my body. I brush my arms off. Glass and blood drip off my fingertips. I shake my head. Back to reality. I look up at my family and nod. I know what I must do.

I glance to the floor at my fallen enemy. They say man's only enemy is himself. I guess I always failed to look at the situation through their eyes. I see now. My eyes are open.

I limp to the kitchen and pull a towel out of a cabinet. I walk back to the fish and pick it up. I look at it one last time.

"I am...so very sorry things turned out this way for us. It's time you go home. It's time you go back to where you're from. It's time to join your family. Farewell my fallen comrade."

I wrap the towel around its taut body and walk out the back door. One gasp of fresh air, and a whole new feeling surrounds me. It's sunny outside. A new day. My father always said tomorrow is another day, a new day. It's true. I've wasted too much to wait until tomorrow. Today is today. Now is now.

I move to the stream and bend down over it. I grab a corner of the towel and let it go, out of my grasp. The fish rolls off into the water. Splash! It sinks down and rises up for a moment. It slowly floats away out of my sight. I sigh as I see it off.

I rise back up and turn toward the house. I squint and smile at the sunlight. It's refreshing. Now it is a new day, a new second, a new chance. As I walk toward the house, leaving the stream behind me, I drop the towel. I stop. I better pick that back up; I'll be needing it.

www.ingramcontent.com/pod-product-compliance
Lightning Source LLC
Chambersburg PA
CBHW030814310726
48980CB00006B/496/J
9780615243368